D0130649

FLORAL STREET

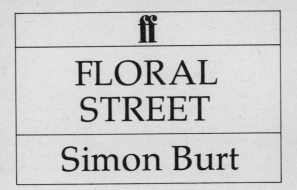

ff

FLORAL STREET

Simon Burt

faber and faber
LONDON · BOSTON

First published in 1986
by Faber and Faber Limited
3 Queen Square London WC1N 3AU

Photoset and printed in Great Britain by
Redwood Burn Limited Trowbridge Wiltshire
All rights reserved

'Floral Street' and 'Welcome' were previously published in *Mae West is Dead*, edited by Adam Mars Jones, Faber and Faber, 1983

British Library Cataloguing in Publication Data

Burt, Simon
Floral street.
I. Title
823'.914[F]   PR6052.U6/

ISBN 0–571–13825–X
ISBN 0–571–13600–1

CONTENTS

WELCOME

The bar closed at two-thirty, by which time the beautiful people had all gone and all that was left was scrag end, and Abel Baker could have some time to himself. Only the truly desperate stayed till three when the lights went up. Abel Baker hated it when the lights went up, and usually stayed in the foyer when they did, chatting with Misha the bouncer, and waiting for Maggie the hat-check girl. You couldn't talk to Maggie till well after three. The desperate and the scrag end kept her too busy. Misha the bouncer was more decorative than functional. He was one of McTeague's cast-offs, and looked stunning in black tie. On the one occasion that Abel Baker could remember that there had been a disturb-ance, a scuffle almost, at reception, Misha had vaulted Maggie's counter and hidden among the coats, leaving Maggie to cope with it. McTeague, as Abel Baker had good cause to know, was gen-erous to his cast-offs. To each according to his level, if not his ca-pacity, which was why Misha was a bouncer and wore black tie, and Abel Baker was a welcomer and had an account at Brown's. At half-past three Misha, Maggie and Abel Baker always went down the street to Oakapple's for breakfast, before each took his separate taxi home. There had been a time when Abel Baker had tried, or hoped, to prevail upon either Misha or Maggie to share his taxi home, but that was before he knew what was what. Lone-liness is loneliness after all, and has its rules, and is not to be tres-passed upon. It was not impossible anyway to find something at Oakapple's if you really had to. There was an established pro-cedure for it, of which from time to time either Misha, or Maggie, or Abel Baker availed themselves. Once eye-contact had been established, and smiles exchanged, the one concerned stood up and said goodbye to the others, and was henceforth invisible. Any further comment or contact was a great breach of tact. It was understood that at that hour of the morning standards were not high. Of the three it was Misha who was most often invisible. He was the youngest, and his appeal, in Abel Baker's eyes at least, the most obvious. Abel Baker left before the others, except on the nights of Misha's invisibility, when Maggie became silent and sullen and stomped off early. Once, leaving shortly afterwards, Abel Baker had seen her leaning against a parking meter, crying, and had passed by on the other side of the street, thinking: What can we do? We are all long past the good Samaritan stage. We all know exactly what we are doing, and could quit tomorrow if we wanted to. It was neither the first nor the last time he had had the thought.

At three-thirty Misha bowed out the last of the scrag end, and closed the door. Maggie came out from behind her counter and joined Misha and Abel Baker in a cigarette.

A busy night, she said.

Not bad, Misha said.

Another glamorous evening, Abel Baker said.

They drew on their cigarettes. From behind Maggie's counter the telephone rang. She answered it, and held out the receiver to Abel Baker.

CMG, she said.

Oh God, Abel Baker said.

He took the receiver and covered the mouthpiece with his hand.

Take a deep breath, Misha said.

Abel Baker raised his eyes to heaven, uncovered the mouthpiece, and spoke.

Hi, he said. Right. Now? OK, I'll be straight down.

He hung up.

An interview, he said. An audience. A vocation.

We'll wait, Misha said.

CMG's office was at the back of the club. Through the restaurant, down the spiral staircase, past the bar, the disco, and the dance-floor. So Abel Baker would have to face the turned up lights after all.

It had been McTeague's idea to keep the décor simple. Let the people provide the colour, he had said. So everything was plain, all cane and stainless steel, and glass and smoked mirrors. White table-cloths, and cool Perspex framed prints clamped on to taut vertical wires. When the lights were down it worked. When the lights were up it looked shabby, the walls stained, the steel and glass finger-marked, the oatmeal carpet drink-splashed and cigarette-burned. Abel Baker crossed the restaurant and went down the staircase with his eyes focused on his feet. The dance-floor was being vacuumed, and the noise echoed in Abel Baker's ears, which were already ringing from the night's exposure to relentless disco. His throat was dry too, after hours of shouting above the music, and he cleared it painfully before he knocked on CMG's door.

CMG was, of course, one of McTeague's cast-offs. The initials stood for Call Me God, a nickname that Maggie had started and now had gained universal acceptance, even from CMG, who had initially showed signs of resentment. There were rumours that McTeague himself had laughed when he had heard it, and what McTeague liked, even from as far away as San Francisco, went.

CMG's office was a biscuit-coloured, windowless cube, furnished with steel and leather deckchairs, potted fig-trees, and two square yards of smoked glass, behind which CMG sat night after night, totting up sheets of figures, and writing letters to McTeague. There were two electric fans on the desk, and a centre punkah. CMG liked to be cool. The effect, as Abel Baker came in from the dance-floor, was like opening a fridge.

Hi, Abel Baker said.

Hello, CMG said, without looking up. I'll be with you in a minute.

You wanted to see me, Abel Baker said.

CMG looked up from his desk.

Oh it's you, he said. Pour yourself a drink. I'll be through here shortly.

No thanks, Abel Baker said. I've had enough. It's been a crowded evening.

Really, CMG said. It was that I wanted to see you about. I won't be long.

Abel Baker sat in a deckchair. He turned up his jacket collar, and hugged himself, and shivered. CMG tapped his pen on his papers. Abel Baker shifted in his chair, and yawned.

I was hoping to make a quick getaway, he said. Like I said, it's been a crowded evening.

None of us is indispensable, CMG said. Like I said, I'll be through here in a minute.

So Abel Baker waited. CMG ran his pen down the margin of his paper, tapped the page when he reached the bottom, and turned over to run his pen down the margin of the other side. He let the paper fall on to the desk top, and screwed the top on to his pen. He tapped his pen on the desk top, and looked across at Abel Baker.

I sometimes wonder, he said, if you understand the nature of our position here.

Abel Baker tipped an eyebrow.

I mean, CMG continued, I am here to run the place. That means I'm in charge. That means what I say goes. You're here to be a welcomer.

In a menial capacity, Abel Baker said.

Sort of in between, CMG said. Neither one thing nor the other. Not floor staff, and not management. Definitely not management.

Like a governess, Abel Baker said. Between floors. Neither staff nor family. I get the picture.

Definitely not management, CMG said. Which means that what I say goes with you too.

Not welcome on either level, Abel Baker said. I get the picture.

I wonder if you do, CMG said. Don't confuse yourself with the people you're paid to welcome. They are the stars. You are the employee. No matter how many of them you know. No matter how smart you are. You still have to do as I say.

I really do get the picture, Abel Baker said.

I've had complaints, CMG said.

Oh, said Abel Baker. Who have I insulted now? It's a week since I spilled a drink over anyone.

It's a week since you scored more than two bottles of champagne a table, said CMG. How you treat your clients is your business, just as long as they come back for more. And they're not coming back. Just look at this.

With the tip of his pen he flipped open a large leather-padded book, span it round, and pushed it towards Abel Baker, who leant forward in his deckchair to receive it.

Complaints, he said. From stateside.

Stateside, Abel Baker said. Dear God, what books have you been reading? Who's been getting these complaints, anyway? You or me?

Well, strictly speaking, me, CMG said. I do run-the place.

Credit where it's due, Abel Baker said.

But I've pinpointed the cause, CMG said. It's in there. Look at it. Who is Mick Dacres, for God's sake? And Karen Goodhue. That book is for names.

So, said Abel Baker, the place is falling off. It's in the nature of things. Mick Dacres is the bass guitarist of a group called Heart-throb. Their record is number thirty-six. Karen Goodhue is a model. She was in last month's *Harper's*.

Like I said, CMG said. That book is for names. Not third-raters and session men.

Fashion moves on, Abel Baker said. That's how clubs work, in case you hadn't noticed. You begin with stars, and end up with stargazers. We had the stars and they've moved on. There isn't a damn thing you or I can do about it.

Unfortunately, CMG said, it's your job to do something about it. And mine to make sure you do. From now on I'm inspecting the Visitor's Book every night. And it's going to look up. Get on the phone. Get your smart friends here. No more Mick Dacres and Karen Goodhue. I want names, and a lot of them. Or you're out.

Now wait a minute, Abel Baker said. I'm just welcomer here. Nobody said anything about touting for trade.

So show me your job description, CMG said.

I shall call McTeague, Abel Baker said.

I dare you, CMG said. I dare you, that's all.

Abel Baker snapped the Visitors' Book shut, and tossed it back across the desk. He extracted himself with difficulty from the deckchair, and stood leaning his hands on the desk.

You're a fucking liar, he said. Complaints. You haven't heard a bloody word.

So you're going to call and find out, CMG said. I'd make damn sure before I risked that if I were you.

Bastard, Abel Baker said.

You're marking the desktop with your hands, CMG said.

What is it? Abel Baker said. What is it that makes you dislike me like this?

Call Me God, CMG said. You think you're unassailable, don't you? That you can go around making up names for people. You think you're God, or something? And I'm supposed not to resent it. To smile and take it. Get your hands off my desk.

Abel Baker put his hands in his pockets, straightened his elbows and hunched his shoulders forward as if standing in the rain. He knew it suited him. He had hundreds of photographs of it suiting him, left over from his days as a model, days before McTeague. He only did it when he felt threatened. It made him look insolent. Frowning against an incipient headache, he turned and walked to the door, and turned and walked back again.

It wasn't me, he said. Who made it up. That wasn't me.

You make me sick, CMG said. With your loose tie. Your turned-up collar. And your floppy hair. Get out of here.

The dance-floor and the spiral staircase were dark when Abel Baker left CMG's office. He felt his way to the stairs and sat on the bottom step with his elbows on his knees and his head in his hands. After a while he bit the back of his left hand hard and clenched his eyes shut. He hated himself in minute particular. The door at the top of the staircase opened and Misha's shadow in a wedge of light flashed on to the wall. Abel Baker unfastened his teeth from his hand.

Dark. Misha's voice called. He must be still in the office.

Abel Baker stood up.

I'm just coming, he said.

Maggie was fretting, Misha said.

Abel Baker ascended the staircase.

Bad? Misha said.

Not good, Abel Baker said. Not the worst, but not good.

He's a fink, Misha said. He's a bastard. Don't let it get you down. He can't help it.

Misha, Abel Baker said, I feel sick.

Misha put his arms around Abel Baker's waist, and walked him through the dining room. The lights were still up, and cane chairs inverted over glass-topped tables aired their ravelled bottoms. The last cleaner unplugged the last vacuum. Abel Baker put his arm around Misha's waist.

Better? Misha said.

Well, over anyway, Abel Baker said. For the moment. Until next time.

Come on, Misha said. I'll buy you a drink.

The next time, Abel Baker said.

Maggie, in the foyer, looked at their linked bodies and said, Oh dear, and twined her arm round Abel Baker's waist from the other side.

What we need, she said, is breakfast. And something frivolous to drink. We'll let Oakapple dream up something special.

Three abreast they negotiated the door. As they left the club dawn was breaking over Curzon Street. They turned their backs to the rising sun, and walked, still linked round Abel Baker's waist, down the street to Oakapple's.

Well, hallelujah! Oakapple said. See who it ain't. The e–ternal tri–angle.

No one had tried to keep the decor simple at Oakapple's. Oakapple herself would have howled with boredom at the suggestion. What she wanted was vulgarity, and noise, and lots of it. Reggae thumped, lights flashed on corrugated tin roofs slung over rattan tables, tropical vegetation – as tropical as Mayfair could manage – burgeoned. One whole wall was given over to the representation of a storm at sunset, with wind-dashed palms and heaping waves. Oakapple, turbaned and wearing what appeared to be some four or five multicoloured bedspreads, presided from a high stool at the bar. She peered at Abel Baker over the top of her bamboo-framed glasses.

Welcome, honey, welcome, you look like shit. What can I press you to?

It was a theory of Oakapple's that the best way to express your personality was through your choice of drink. And she liked your personality to be complicated. She liked to mix cocktails, and was never happier than when shaking a Bosom Caresser, or a Sloe Comfortable Screw Up Against The Wall, or balancing layers of subtle liquors one on top of the other into a Rainbow Sundae. Misha usually humoured her and ordered some towering and deadly confection. Maggie and Abel Baker pleaded their livers and stuck to lager. Lager depressed Oakapple.

Tonight, Oakapple honey, Maggie said. We need you. Tonight is the pits. Tonight is the ass. Tonight is the fat end of the wedge.

Ain't it always, honey, Oakapple said. Take a look around you, and see what the tide washed up. Nothin' but the mackintosh brigade. Nothin' stronger than a brandy Alexander in the place. How's tricks your end of the market?

Don't ask, Abel Baker said. Just don't ask. Therein is the root of the trouble.

We need help, Misha said. To get through the night. Your help, Oakapple honey. Tonight we are giving you free rein.

No lagers? Oakapple asked.

No lagers, Abel Baker said.

So-ho! Oakapple said. Sit down, honeys, and prepare yourselves. Oakapple's going to fix you something that will blow your head away!

I sure hope so, Abel Baker said.

They sat at a table in a corner by the bar, and surveyed the scene.

I can see what she meant, Misha said. There's not much here for the heart's hunger. I wonder which is the brandy Alexander.

So what did CMG want? Maggie asked.

He doesn't like me, Abel Baker said.

So what's new! Maggie said. So who would have guessed? So what can he do about it?

He's out to get me, Abel Baker said.

How? Maggie said. Just how can he do that? McTeague's on your side.

McTeague! Misha said. McTeague's on everybody's side.

Misha honey, Abel Baker said. Tonight you are showing a wisdom beyond your years.

I sure wish I could see that brandy Alexander, Misha said.

It doesn't mean anything, Maggie said. Oakapple just bullied him, that's all. He probably doesn't even know what he's drinking.

Nevertheless, Misha said.

Nevertheless! Maggie said. Neverthebloodyless! You sound like CMG.

Abel Baker leant his head back against the wall and closed his eyes. Maggie and Misha bickered above the sound of reggae. If, Abel Baker thought, people go on and on behaving in the same way, it must mean they like it, mustn't it? You just don't go on and on doing something if you don't like it, do you?

Oakapple swept up to their table, bearing a tray of three mountainous cocktails, each topped with cream, and cherries, and dusted with coconut.

The answer to all your prayers, she said. Peacock-hued sweet oblivion in a glass.

Better set up the next one, Maggie said. There's a lot to forget.

Honey, Oakapple said, you drink two of these, I'll pay the bill myself!

That good, huh? Abel Baker said.

Oakapple, Misha said. Which is the brandy Alexander?

Forget it, honey, Oakapple said. You're not for him. Oakapple can tell these things. You're too young and stupid. He likes the maturer man.

All this from a brandy Alexander? Abel Baker said.

Believe me, Oakapple said. I can tell. He likes the maturer man. With brains.

Nevertheless, Maggie said.

Neverthebloodyless, Misha said. Where is he, Oakapple?

Other side of the bar, Oakapple said. Blue velvet trousers, and one of those Walkman machines. My music ain't for him. Don't say I didn't warn you.

Show me, Misha said.

Listen, honey, Oakapple said. He likes them with brains. I told you. What's he going to think of a guy can't even find him by himself? Now, I've got a bar to tend to.

Back at the bar, she hoisted herself on to a stool, caught Abel Baker's eye and winked, jerking her head in the direction of the other side of the room.

You! she mouthed. You! Go get him.

Abel Baker smiled and sipped his drink, and shook his head.

Misha stood up.

OK then, he said. I'll go and check him out.

See you then, Maggie said.

Not too soon, I hope, Misha said.

Good luck, Abel Baker said. Don't forget your drink.

By the time Misha had disappeared round the edge of the bar, Maggie had downed her drink and was signalling to Oakapple for another. Oakapple shook her head.

Don't you worry, honey, she shouted. He'll be back.

Maggie thumped her glass on the table.

Silly bitch, she said. What do I care if he comes back or not. I want another drink.

She sniffed, and glared at Abel Baker with tearbright eyes.

I want another fucking drink, she said. Shit! Why do I never get what I want?

She stood up.

I'm going for a piss, she said.

Abel Baker finished his drink. After a few minutes Misha came back and sat down.

Where's Maggie? he said.

He waved his empty glass at Oakapple and gestured round the table. Oakapple got off her barstool and mixed another round of drinks. Maggie came back as she brought them to the table.

Oakapple honey, Maggie said. You're not a silly bitch really. None of us knows what we'd do without you.

Go home straight after work is what you'd do without me, Oakapple said. Ain't nowhere else to go. Don't forget now. You drink these, I pay for them.

Abel Baker felt as if the floor was rippling under his chair. Maggie leaned her hand on Misha's shoulder as she sat down.

I daren't think what this drink is, Abel Baker said. It tastes like syrup of figs. I think I might go to the lavatory for a while.

On his way there he saw the brandy Alexander, and they exchanged smiles. Definitely not English, Abel Baker decided. French maybe, or Spanish, judging by the clothes. A nice, shy face. I like the way he looks out from under his eyebrows. In the lavatory he plunged his face into a basinful of cold water, and checked himself in the mirror. He twitched his tie, and ran his fingers through his hair.

Oh well, he said to his reflection. Coming, ready or not.

The brandy Alexander was sitting with his back to the lavatory door. Abel Baker went up behind him, and touched his hair. The brandy Alexander turned round. Good eyes, Abel Baker thought. My God, he must be all of nineteen.

Hi, he said. What are you listening to?

The brandy Alexander took off his headphones.

Comment? he said. Sorry. I did not hear.

I said hello, Abel Baker said. And what are you listening to?

Monteverdi, the brandy Alexander said. Hello. Please, sit down and join me.

I have a better idea, Abel Baker said. Why don't we both sit down somewhere else? Like in a taxi. Back to my place.

The brandy Alexander put his headphones round his neck.

OK, he said.

He reached into his pocket and turned his tape-recorder off.

I don't need music now, he said. You are enough.

23

Maggie and Misha were still sitting at their table as Abel Baker took the brandy Alexander out. Neither nodded, or smiled, or waved. Misha took up Abel Baker's drink, and swallowed it.

You like music? the brandy Alexander said, in the taxi. What sort of music do you like?

Monteverdi, Abel Baker said.

The brandy Alexander leaned his head on Abel Baker's shoulder.

Tired? Abel Baker said.

Go on lying to me, the brandy Alexander said. I like it.

I do, Abel Baker said. I have the records at home.

The brandy Alexander nuzzled Abel Baker's ear. Abel Baker noticed with horror that he was wearing sandals and blue nylon socks.

Tell me what you do, the brandy Alexander said.

I welcome, Abel Baker said. I am a welcomer. I work in a club, and whenever anyone famous comes in, I rush up and make a fuss of them, and ask them to sign a book. It makes them feel loved.

Make me feel loved, the brandy Alexander said.

Do you mind if I wait till we get home? Abel Baker said. I'm not good in taxis.

Hold me, the brandy Alexander said.

Abel Baker put his arm round the brandy Alexander's shoulder. The brandy Alexander inserted his hand between Abel Baker's thighs. The taxi pulled up outside Abel Baker's flat.

So, the brandy Alexander said, as Abel Baker showed him into the sitting room. Where are all the Monteverdi records?

Make yourself at home, Abel Baker said. Sit down while I put one on.

The brandy Alexander sat on the sofa, and Abel Baker put on the 1610 Vespers.

There, he said. I told you.

He knelt on the floor between the brandy Alexander's legs. The brandy Alexander leaned forward to be kissed. His eyes were half closed, and his eyeballs were turned up under his lids, so that all

24

Abel Baker could see of them was two white crescents in the middle of his face. Abel Baker kissed him, and ran an exploratory hand under his T-shirt. The boy's shoulders were rough to the touch, and proved, on closer inspection, to be speckled with innumerable blackheads. Nevertheless, Abel Baker persisted in his embraces.

At half past one the next afternoon Abel Baker woke to an empty space in the bed beside him. He had had trouble sleeping. The brandy Alexander had been disposed to be cuddlesome, and none of Abel Baker's devices – twitching legs, falling asleep and waking up with a jerk, even a determined move to the other side of the bed – had been able to dissuade him. He wanted to fall asleep in Abel Baker's arms. He wanted to rest a tousled head on Abel Baker's chest, and every now and then raise a fuddled face for a kiss. Abel Baker had lain sleepless, cross, and increasingly hot, till eventually the brandy Alexander had slept, and he could disengage himself. Even so his sleep had been punctuated by mumbled endearments, sleep-furred kisses, and palping hands. Now he surveyed the empty pillow next to him with relief, and would have slept again had not a furtive noise from the sitting room made him sit up and think: Oh God, he's stealing something.

Swiftly Abel Baker enumerated to himself the small moveable objects in his sitting room and mentally adjusted himself to their absence. His wallet, he knew, was nearly empty, indeed had cost more than was ever in it, but his cheque book and credit cards were on his desk. He was running over in his head the drill for reporting their loss when the brandy Alexander, clothed and coated for the street, came back into the bedroom.

Ah, he said, you are awake. You slept well?

As you see, Abel Baker said. I slept beautifully.

The brandy Alexander took Abel Baker's hand and sat on the bed.

I too, he said. Very fine. But now I must go.

Abel Baker threw back the sheets.

No, the brandy Alexander said. Stay. Go back to sleep. I must go. I will say goodbye now.

Abel Baker stood up.

No, the brandy Alexander said. Lie down again. I don't want to disturb you. I will let myself out.

He took Abel Baker in his arms.

You are a good man, he said. You gave me a good night. Thank you. Now get back into bed.

Abel Baker lay down, and the brandy Alexander tucked the sheets round him.

Sleep now, he said, and kissed Abel Baker's eyes closed.

Goodbye, he said.

Abel Baker waited till he heard the front door close, then got up and went to survey the sitting room. Nothing was missing. His wallet, cheque book, passport, everything was where it should be. The Monteverdi record had been taken off the turntable and returned to its box, which lay on the coffee table holding down a note, which Abel Baker sat on the sofa to read.

If one day, he read, you come to Paris remember this fellow you cross the time of a night. He lives in the 18th, and likes Monteverdi. If you have nothing else to do than to remember a night on the sweating catacombs of London, just come to him. Sure he'd be happy to see you again. I give you his address.

His name was: Dominique Chaussure.
And he lives: 8, passage Daunay
                75018 Paris.

Chaussure! Abel Baker said. Oh God. Dominic Shoe.

He folded the note carefully and put it in his wallet. If ever, he thought, if ever by some remote chance I might be seduced into thinking myself a nice guy, all I shall have to do is take out that note and read it.

He made himself a cup of coffee and went back to bed. He smoked a cigarette and stared at the ceiling. He dozed and woke to cold coffee. He looked at his watch. Three o'clock. Early morning in San Francisco. He reached for the phone and dialled.

Hello, McTeague's voice said.

Abel Baker covered the mouthpiece with his hand.

Hello, McTeague said again. Hello.

Abel Baker lay the phone down on the bed. McTeague's voice went on saying hello impassively and at intervals, until Abel Baker hung up.

Misha, even more stunning in taut blue denim than in black tie, threw his coat over the counter to Maggie, and blew Abel Baker a kiss.

Give us a break, Maggie said. It's your night off.

Can't help it, Misha said. Here's where the action is. Can't stay away.

See you later maybe, Maggie said. Will you be coming to Oakapple's?

I hope not, Misha said. I sure as hell hope not. I don't know why I keep going to that place.

The club door opened, and Abel Baker poised himself, flashing a welcoming smile, but it was only an early bit of scrag end, so he relaxed again. Misha passed and tweaked his cheek.

Have a good night, old love, he said.

Abel Baker went and leaned on Maggie's counter.

How do you feel? he said. She sure as hell mixes a mean cocktail.

I got home in the end, Maggie said.

Misha? Abel Baker said.

We walked, Maggie said. We couldn't get a taxi so we walked. If you can call it that. We propped each other up.

Oh well, Abel Baker said. And here we all are again.

Why? Maggie said. I wish I knew that. Why the fuck do we go on doing it?

We are all, Abel Baker thought, caught in a trap with no door. We could leave, walk out, tomorrow. All it takes is a phone call to San Francisco.

This observation, though comforting, though giving him the courage to stay where he was, Abel Baker judged premature, unwelcome even, in Maggie's case, so he kept it to himself. The door was opening anyway, and he sprang forward.

Mick! he said. Karen! Hi! Come in! Welcome!

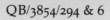

QB/3854/294 & 6

Despite all the precautions taken by his friends, Professor Mehring was called out of the ranks during roll-call. When the punishment squad, performing its exercise, began to thin out, Professor Mehring was seized by an extraordinary will to live and start 1 running like a madman. Lalka observed this and, when a quarter of the prisoners had fallen, made the exercise go on to see how long the old man, running a few yards behind the others, could hold out.

He yelled – If you catch up with them, your life is saved.

And he gave the order to whip on the survivors. The survivors faltered and slowed down in order to help the professor; but the blows redoubled, making them stumble, shredding their clothes, covering their faces with blood. Blinded with blood, reeling with pain, they again speeded up. The professor, who had gained a little ground, saw them pull away from him again and threw his arms forward, as if to grasp the other prisoners, as if to plead with them. He stumbled once, then a second time; his tortured body seemed to fall apart; he tried once more to recover his balance, then, all at once, stiffened and collapsed in the dust. When the Germans drew near, they saw a thread of blood flowing from his mouth. Professor Mehring was dead.

Thank you, my dear Carlos, for the books. If we are not entirely out of touch here, far from the centre of things as we by necessity are, it is due largely to your kindness. I wonder if you read any of them before you sent them on. In case you did not, I attach a quotation for your interest. I am, as you know, as keen a student of the literature inspired by our work here as the circumstances of our isolation and your generosity permit, but I must admit that I am not acquainted with the primary source of the quotation – a study of Treblinka by one Jean-François Steiner – and I would be very grateful if you could track it down and forward it to me here.

I came across the quotation in the volume of essays called *Language and Silence* by another Steiner – George, I assume no relation – of whom I had not previously heard, and again I would be grateful if you could furnish me with further examples of his work, as I find that, although he manifests ample evidence of those prejudices usual among those who are not actively involved in our work, his mind chimes admirably with my own. He has, of course, a far greater gift of words than I, and an unfortunate habit of what I can only describe as masturbation of the superego in connection with our work, a sort of delicate probing and palping of the conscience until it secretes delicious remorse, but, with a shift of emphasis here and there, I find his thought inspiring. Another of the essays in his collection is entitled 'Dying Is An Art'. You see, my dear Carlos, along how parallel a line of development with our own the thought of our opponents runs. I shall also need, for reasons that will become apparent, another musician.

Immediately on reading the quotation, although it was evident that the circumstances of the experiment were by no means ideal, I decided that something of the same sort would not be out of place here. I would take care, of course, that what I regarded as the less desirable aspects of the original case would not be duplicated. The quoted case has all the hallmarks of spontaneity that would disbar it from serious consideration here, where more controlled circumstances are our aim. Although, for instance, the treatment of his fellow runners is a nicely judged piece of improvisation, I can only regard the choice of Professor Mehring as subject, a man obviously – if I read the passage correctly, and accurate deduction is difficult, out of context as the passage is – not up to the physical demands of the experiment, as particularly infelicitous. A stronger or more healthy man would make the experiment, testing as it does the nice balance between fear and loyalty, companionship and libido, more valid, and therefore more interesting.

For my experiment, then, I chose two men who are, insofar as it is possible here, strong and healthy, and, with the same proviso, mutually attached. They were, I am told, friends in the outside world, and indeed were arrested at the same time, in the same place, and on the same charge. Furthermore, a rare occurrence indeed, and one which has caused me to request stronger vigilance on the part of base administration, as it should, as you know, never have been permitted, they travelled here in the same compartment, which accounts for the closeness of their serial numbers. I chose internees no. QB/3854/294 & 6, or, though I am sure your filing system is as good as mine, Dr Luis Reutemann, formerly lecturer in Musicology at the University of San Felipe, and Dr Guillermo Powell, formerly lecturer in Behavioural Psychology at the same institution. They are both men of cultivated background and for that reason, as I am fond of intellectual discussion, and, as you know, passionately addicted to jazz, of which Dr Reutemann was a skilful practitioner, have been my orderlies here at the villa for the last eight months, and have, as a result, enjoyed privileged status.

(I will admit, privately, that this privilege, leading as it inevitably did, though I myself have done nothing to encourage them, to unwarrantable assumptions of security, did not decrease my inclination to choose them. I must emphasize again that I mention this fact privately, as I am not particularly proud of it, evidencing as it does an undesirably unscientific approach to the matter in hand. I mention it merely in passing, as one of the vagaries of spirit perhaps inevitable in one of my isolated position and, having noted it, you may be sure that I will guard against it in the future. Fortunately it has no bearing on the present case.)

When I informed them of my decision and choice, as I did after having asked Dr Powell to read and comment on the quoted passage during the course of our habitual evening discussion while Dr Reutemann played the piano, on the 27th of last month, they both evinced at first signs of surprise and incredulity. I did my best to assure them of the seriousness of my intentions, and sent them to their quarters to prepare themselves for the experiment, which I intended to put in train on the Monday of the following week.

My first plan was to use the main camp assembly area as a

course, and to observe the proceedings from the upper balcony of my villa, but this struck me later as being undesirable for a variety of reasons. First, the presence or proximity of the main body of internees, who would of necessity be ranked in the area during an undertaking of this sort. As a general rule I have no objection to their participation, but on this occasion I felt that their presence would only detract from, or weaken my concentration on, what I intended to be a major piece of work. Second, it was too ordinary a location. The main assembly area is used for a whole series of petty daily events, and this could not but introduce an element of the quotidian where I least desired it. Third, and I think most important, I was by no means pleased by my own distance from the affair. It seemed to me that to remove myself to the position of detached spectator, as, even with the aid of field glasses, I could not help doing if I were to take up my post on my balcony, was to deny one of the seminal theses of modern science, that is the essential involvement of the observer. It is, as is well known, impossible for the observer to have no effect on the observed system, and conversely I have always held that the observed system itself should be in as close a relation as possible to the observer. I chose, then, for the course the area between the inner and outer perimeter fences of the main camp, a distance of some two kilometres, which, with the removal of the cross-wires at the gate, and the stationing of a monitoring guard at intervals of fifty metres along the inner fence, could be turned into a very functional track. I myself could be driven round the outer fence in a Land Rover, and keep pace with the runners.

My main preoccupation, on the morning of the experiment itself, was that I could not be sure of the active co-operation of the two subjects. Possibly, despite my repeated assurances to the contrary, they might still entertain some doubt – and here I must ask you to bear in mind what I have already mentioned, namely the unwontedly privileged position they had enjoyed under my, as it were, protection – some doubt as to the seriousness of my purpose. It would be a great pity if the experiment were to be marred in any way by their expecting some last-minute clemency on my

part. Or worse still if some residual notion of honour or dignity –
they were, after all, educated men – might prevent their taking
part with all the enthusiasm I wished; if, for example, they were
simply to run towards each other, join hands, and turn to face the
guns of the guards, as I have heard that many of the more misguided of our opponents have done when faced with unavoidable
defeat at our hands. I thought of various courses of action that
might avoid such a contingency. I thought that perhaps I might
arrange some sort of trial run, witnessed by the two subjects, that
would convince them that non-participation was useless, some
sort of charade that would convince them to make every effort to
ensure the experiment's smooth running. And I must admit that I
found it difficult, if not in the last analysis impossible, to decide
what form this trial run or charade might take, to strike a balance
between the firmness that would assure them that I was in earn-
est, and the elasticity that would allow them some sort of hope
of survival and thereby avoid forcing them to commit themselves
to the dignity of inevitable defeat. And, of course, which would
not reduce to the level of anti-climax the experiment itself. Ultimately however it came to me that this suspense of mine was in
fact an intimate part of the experiment, and that I could not
remove my anxiety in this connection without jeopardizing the in-
tegrity of the whole undertaking. I too would have to take my
chance along with the rest. In a word, I would have to wait and
see what happened. Anything else would be prejudicing the outcome unduly in my own favour.

To come then to the experiment: At noon, as usual, I had the
whole camp fall in in the main assembly area, supervised on this
occasion by the whole guard force, excepting only those I had
already posted round the course, and two sergeants to conduct
the subjects to the gate where the experiment was to begin. I
made no announcement to the assembly. I simply conducted roll
call and inspection in the usual way, and proceeded to my Land
Rover, which was positioned outside the fence. From the Land
Rover I explained the rules to the participants one last time: Dr
Powell was stationed twenty metres to the front of Dr Reute-

mann. When they heard the sound of the starting pistol they were
to run. Should Dr Reutemann succeed in catching up with Dr
Powell, Dr Powell would be immediately shot. Should he not, he
would be shot himself. Should either of them at any time drop out
of the race both would be shot. Bearing in mind the preoccu-
pations I have already described you can imagine with what trepi-
dation I pulled the trigger of the starting pistol. I need not have
worried. Both subjects sprinted so swiftly forward that my driver
had some difficulty in keeping abreast of them over the bumpy
terrain outside the wire.

Both Dr Reutemann and Dr Powell were in late middle age and,
although of a sedentary disposition which their months as my
orderlies had done little to change, both relatively fit and stout-
hearted, as such things are measured here. They maintained a
high speed for the first circuit without obvious discomfort, and
managed a second with only a slight diminution. I was surprised
by how little the distance between them varied. I had judged my
subjects well. By half way through the third circuit both were flag-
ging visibly, Dr Reutemann perhaps a thought more than Dr
Powell by a metre or so, and for the rest of the circuit the distance
between them fluctuated, as first one then the other put on a burst
of speed, but again not significantly until the middle of the fifth
circuit when Dr Reutemann stumbled and almost fell, and would
have lost ground irretrievably had not Dr Powell taken advantage
of the mishap and slowed down for a moment. Dr Reutemann
quickly righted himself and both ran on. By the seventh circuit
both subjects were breathing stertorously and had reduced speed
almost to a jog. I ordered the guards to cock their rifles, and speed
increased temporarily, but after a further eighty metres or so I was
forced to order the guards to fire at their heels to keep up their
effort. Even so, by the eighth circuit, still with the original
distance between them more or less maintained, they were
unable to do more than walk. My dear Carlos, I would need the
pen of a Steiner to describe my emotions during that desperate
walk. By now I was shouting encouragement indiscriminately. I
cared nothing for the outcome of the race. I only wanted it to con-

tinue. Dr Powell was obviously in extreme pain. Bent forward almost double at the waist, his breathing roaring in his throat, his arms flailing, he hobbled forward. Dr Reutemann was in an even worse condition. He breathed in anguished intermittent gulps, and blood trickled from his nose and ears. I expected his collapse at any moment. But it was Dr Powell who fell first. Towards the end of the tenth circuit, having covered a distance of nearly twenty kilometres, a titanic performance, you must admit, for one in his condition, he stopped, coughed out a large quantity of blood, and fell on to his face. His legs still worked spasmodically, but it was obvious that he was beyond further effort. Dr Reutemann threw himself forward. Arms stretched out in front of him he staggered across the intervening distance. But, five metres from the prone body of Dr Powell, he himself fell to his knees. Centimetre by centimetre he crawled towards his fellow subject's feet. A metre away he fell on his face, but still managed to inch his way forward until, at last, his hand on Dr Powell's very ankle, he too was incapable of further movement. I administered the *coup de grâce* myself.

And now, of course, in the quiet of the night, I have to ask myself what conclusions can be drawn from all this. On the whole, I must confess that I am disappointed. Only for a short while, after the excitement and uncertainty attendant on the start of the experiment had worn off, was I moved. For a moment, during my subjects' tortured walk, my heart was in my mouth. The tension between them was so nicely judged. But the very niceness of the judgement contained the seeds of disillusionment, and little now remains of that surge of emotion. Worse, I begin to question the validity of my initial premise: that the choice of so sick a man as Professor Mehring was a mistake. As I have said, there was at no time till the very end any significant diminution in the distance between the two runners. They both simply ran until they could run no more. Maybe I am becoming jaded. Maybe I am no longer after all these years up to the demands of my position. I am no longer by any means young, and the bumpy drive in the Land Rover upset me. I feel in a way cheated.

37

Although I have long held that contrary to what is usually stated the true landmarks in one's life are physical – I well remember, for instance, the agony of my first baldness – I expected more of this experiment than it delivered. Now that the excitement, such as it was, has died down, only physical sensation remains. My legs have been bothering me for a long time, and nodules are appearing on my calves. I can no longer ignore the fact that I suffer from a painful and shameful condition of the anus. How futile it is to try to measure up to the giants of the past. I shall take care that any part I take in future experiments will be a less active one.

ANYONE ELSE WOULD LEARN

Coop! Coop! Coop!

Aunt Dorcas sang, as she left Uncle Matthew and came towards us over the field.

Suey! Suey! Suey!

It was a hot day in July, but it could as easily have been a cold day in December or a blustery day in March. The routine would have been the same.

My God, my mother said. You'd think she was calling in the cows.

Coop! Coop! Coop!

Aunt Dorcas sang again.

Trotwood stood still and pricked up her ears. She looked over her shoulder at my aunt, bent to crop a mouthful of grass, and looked up again. Her ears were slightly too long. Even pricked to their fullest they looked floppy.

If she catches her, my mother said. If she just walks right up and catches her and says all you need is gentleness and a bloody way with bloody animals, I will not be responsible for my actions.

I once found Aunt Dorcas on her back in the barn, sprawling in cowshit and spilled milk. The tethered cow that had just kicked her off the milking stool chewed cud and stared at the wall. Aunt Dorcas laughed.

Suey! Suey! Suey!

Aunt Dorcas plucked a tuft of grass and held it out on the palm of her hand.

Trotwood took a few paces towards her.

I knew it, my mother said. I bloody knew it.

Aunt Dorcas was not my aunt. In the old days she had helped around the farm. Now she was my uncle's housekeeper. I called her Aunt.

It was already hot when I woke up.

41

I could see Trotwood from my bedroom window.

She was standing at the edge of the chestnut grove in the middle of the field, twitching her tail and shaking her head against the flies.

My father knocked on the door.

Breakfast, he said. Ready?

Trotwood was my reward. My father bought her for me when I won my scholarship to Hales. Except for her ears she was perfect. Concave-faced, feathery-fetlocked, shaggy-maned and -tailed, barrel-girthed. During the holidays I rode her every day.

Jeremy? my father said. It's eight o'clock.

Every day after breakfast I would collect her from the small paddock at the back of the house, and we would spend the day exploring woods and downs.

Coming, I said. I'm just getting dressed.

Quick now, my father said. Busy day.

It was the first day of the holidays.

I pushed the window right up, leaned out, and clicked my tongue at Trotwood, but she ignored me.

During term-time she lived in the huge tree-lined field at the front of the house. Which was a problem. Trotwood did not like to be caught.

I got out of my pyjamas and into my clothes.

It was all right when she was in the small paddock. I could manage then. It was quite easy to edge her into a corner, avoid her heels, and slip the halter over her floppy ears. Sometimes she would bite. Sometimes she would drag her head away, and I would walk her quietly round the field until I had her cornered again.

The big front field was another matter. At the beginning of every holiday it took all of us to corner, let alone catch, her.

I could hear my mother from the top of the stairs, so I stopped half way down, and sat and waited for her to stop.

My mother is not good in the mornings.

I have seen my mother's world dissolve into panic because the salt was not in its accustomed place on the breakfast trolley.

The dining-room door was ajar. My father said something too quiet for me to hear. My mother didn't stop.

I sat on the stairs and waited.

When I went into the dining room my mother and father were sitting at the table drinking coffee.

I fixed myself a bowl of cereal.

Always the same, my mother said.

I stopped my spoon half way to my mouth, and put it back on the plate.

My father sipped his coffee with tight lips.

Time after time, my mother said.

I lifted my spoon.

Anyone else, my mother said, would learn.

I put my spoon down again.

Why not you? my mother said. Every time the same.

I tried lifting my spoon again, but my mother hadn't finished.

Anyone else, she said. Anyone else would keep her in the small paddock all the time and be done with it.

I stared at my suspended spoon, hoping that my father would say nothing.

You know it's too small, he said. There isn't enough room, enough grass.

Not you, my mother said. Not us. Oh no. We have to do things the hard way.

I lifted my spoon to my mouth.

Time after time, my mother said. The whole bloody day trailing round and round the field.

I put my spoon down again.

The next time I went to lift it my mother knocked it out of my hand.

How dare you, she said. It's your bloody animal, and all you can do is freeze every time I speak.

I picked up my spoon and sat staring at my plate.

Eat your breakfast, my father said.

My mother started again. We both waited for her to stop. I ate my cereal. My father drank his coffee.

43

After breakfast my father went out round the farm, and my mother and I made the beds. We stretched the sheets taut into hospital corners. We lay carefully folded nightwear under plumped pillows. We twitched at the corners of bedspreads. Then I sat in the drawing room for a while, and read, and thought of Trotwood in her field swishing away the flies.

My father came back from his rounds at eleven o'clock, and we all set out for the field.

The technique was simple.

We spread out until there was as much space between us as a quick dash would cover, and walked slowly towards Trotwood. My father held out and shook a tray of oats and made encouraging noises.

Trotwood waited till we were about twenty yards away, then turned and walked off.

Slowly we followed her round and round the field, gently pressing her towards the edge.

This took a long time. I held Trotwood's halter behind my back.

Once we had achieved the edge of the field, we walked along it, still careful to keep our distance, closing Trotwood into the corner. There she turned to face us, and we moved in.

I brought out the halter and held it so that I could slip it over her head. My father held out the tray of oats.

When we were about ten yards away Trotwood dashed forward into the space between my mother and me.

Grab her! my mother shouted.

I threw myself at her, and landed heavily on my stomach just clear of her hind legs.

Trotwood cantered to the chestnut grove. I stood up and leaned my hands on my knees, gulping for air.

When I had recovered we spread out again, and set out for the middle of the field as before.

Trotwood stood in the middle of the grove. When we reached the edge she tossed her head, took a few steps backwards, and was still again.

Talk to her, my father said.

I clicked my tongue.

We walked towards her through the trees.

I clicked my tongue again.

My father held out the tray of oats, and Trotwood leaned her head forward and blew through her lips.

We all held our arms open wide and walked towards her. She turned and walked off into the open field, and we followed her round and round again.

This time we got her cornered by the gate.

Talk to her, my father said.

I clicked my tongue.

Say something to her, my father said.

What shall I say? I said.

We moved closer in.

Trotwood had her back to us.

I don't know, my father said. She's your horse. What do you usually say to her? Sweet nothings.

We spread our arms out wide.

I couldn't think of anything to say.

There, there, my mother said. There, there.

Trotwood, my father said. Trotwood.

We were very close by now. My mother stretched forward and patted Trotwood's hind quarters.

There, she said. Good girl.

I brought out the halter.

Trotwood didn't move.

Good girl, my mother said.

My father stood still.

My mother patted Trotwood's quarters again and walked slowly up her flank, patting and whispering.

Good girl, she said. Good girl.

She patted Trotwood's neck.

There, she whispered. There.

Very gently she took hold of a hank of Trotwood's mane. Very gently she stroked Trotwood's nose. Very carefully she turned to me and winked at the halter.

I took a step forward. And another. I stroked Trotwood's nose with the halter.

There, my mother said. Good girl.

Trotwood span round and raced for the space between my father and the gate.

My mother held on to her mane and ran beside her.

Trotwood broke into a canter.

My mother still held on. Her feet went from under her and she was dragged along the ground, but still she didn't let go.

My father and I ran after her.

Bitch! my mother shouted. Bitch!

Then she let go and fell on her face. My father helped her up.

Bitch! she screamed. Bitch!

She flung her arms round my father. My father stroked her hair. My mother trembled and gasped.

There there, my father said. It's all right. There there.

I hate it, my mother said. I hate it. I can't stand it.

I know, my father said.

He was still holding his tray of oats in one hand while his other stroked my mother's hair.

I know, he said. There, there. It will be all right.

My mother hugged him and was quiet.

It never has been, she said.

I just stood there, holding the halter.

My mother let my father go. She brushed dirt and grass from her front.

Never, she said.

She wiped tears from her face with the back of her hand.

What must I look like? she said.

You always look beautiful to me, my father said.

My mother turned and followed Trotwood across the field.

Always, my father said.

What good does that do? my mother said over her shoulder. We've got a horse to catch.

We spread out and followed Trotwood round and round the field again.

*

Coop! Coop! Coop!

We had been in the field for two hours.

Trotwood was sweating. Her nostrils dilated as she breathed.

Aunt Dorcas was good with animals. They lifted her up. They made her laugh.

My father's lips were set tight. My mother spoke quietly and slowly.

I shall hit her, she said. I swear I shall hit her.

Uncle Matthew leaned on the gate. He waved at me. I smiled, and waved back.

Trotwood stood and looked at Aunt Dorcas.

Uncle Matthew only came to see us rarely nowadays. He dropped in unannounced, and dropped out again.

Well, my father said. It will save time if she does catch her.

Christ! my mother said.

Trotwood lifted her head and whinnied.

Suey! Suey! Suey! my aunt sang.

I don't believe it, my mother said. She's going to.

Uncle Matthew was my father's elder brother. The farm was half his. He had a weak heart. When he lived with us he took me for a drive every Sunday morning. We would stop at a pub and he would buy me a cider, which I drank in the car.

Trotwood walked up to Aunt Dorcas and took the tuft of grass from her palm. Aunt Dorcas held her by the forelock.

There, she said. All you need is gentleness.

My mother ran across and punched her hard on the bust.

Trotwood flung back her head, jerked free of Aunt Dorcas and galloped away.

My mother pummelled Aunt Dorcas's chest and shoulders.

I hate you, she shouted. I hate you.

Aunt Dorcas took a step backwards. My mother flailed her arms, then stood still, panting.

Well, Aunt Dorcas said. And you are supposed to be Mrs Armstrong.

Dorcas, my uncle called. Come away.

47

Yes, my mother said. Yes. I am. And wouldn't you like to be?

I looked at my father. He was looking at his tray of oats. I looked across the field at Uncle Matthew.

Dorcas, he said again. Come away.

My mother shouted at him.

Yes, she said. Go away. You are not welcome here.

Uncle Matthew climbed the gate and walked over to us.

Not welcome, my mother said. You never were. Go away. Take her and go away.

My father went to my mother and put his hand on her shoulder. She shrugged it off.

Always, she said. You always hated me. Right back at the beginning you always mocked me. Go away.

Uncle Matthew just kept on walking.

When I was pregnant even, my mother said. And feeling awful. All you did was mock me.

Uncle Matthew came to a halt in front of her.

You hate me, my mother said. And I hate you.

She turned to Aunt Dorcas.

And you too, she said.

She turned to my father. Then to me.

And you, she said. And you. I hate you all. Go away. All of you.

We all just looked at her.

All of you, she said. Go on. Go away. Leave me alone.

Pull yourself together, Uncle Matthew said.

My mother lifted her hands above her head. I thought she was going to hit Uncle Matthew too.

Stop it, Aunt Dorcas said. Matthew, stop it.

Uncle Matthew didn't move. My mother took a deep breath and dropped her hands.

I'm sorry, she said. I think I'd like to go in now.

Dorcas, my father said.

Aunt Dorcas put her arm round my mother's shoulder.

There, she said. Come on. We'll go in.

My mother put her arm round Aunt Dorcas's waist and leaned her head on her shoulder.

My father, my uncle and I watched as Aunt Dorcas led my mother away over the field and into the house.

My uncle is a happy man. He moves lightly and quickly. He moves his arms a lot and throws himself around when he talks.

Now then, he said. Let's get this horse caught.

We walked Trotwood round and round the field.

Look at you, my uncle said. Look at the two of you.

My father's lips were now so tight you could hardly see them.

Relax, my uncle said. Enjoy.

He ran towards Trotwood.

Come on horse, he said. Come on, horse.

Trotwood ran straight into a corner and turned towards us.

You've got to be quick, my uncle said. You've got to be firm. Go on. Get her.

My father set out towards Trotwood. She fidgeted, and backed on to the fence.

Uncle Matthew and I followed my father. My father walked quicker and quicker.

He went right up to Trotwood and took hold of her mane.

There, Uncle Matthew said. I told you.

He pushed me forward.

Go on, he said. It's your horse.

I went to Trotwood and put the halter over her head.

Got you, cabbage ears, my uncle said.

My father let go the mane.

Uncle Matthew assumed the pose of a javelin thrower.

Victory, he shouted. Victory!

He ran up and loosed his imaginary javelin. At the last second he closed his hand into a fist and punched Trotwood on the nose.

Trotwood reared back hard on to the fence, then pushed forward, knocking Uncle Matthew over, and dragging me with her by the halter.

I held on as long as I could, but I soon had to let go.

I stood looking after her.

My father ran past me.

Trotwood galloped up to the gate, and turned and galloped round the field.

My father stopped running just by the chestnut grove. He stood for a while, then leaned back, and flung his tray of oats as hard as he could into the air.

I stepped back and bumped into Uncle Matthew. Together we watched the tray as it flew in a scatter of oats high, high, high over the trees.

FELLOW PASSENGERS

*After her husband died Ann Upnor took to dancing by herself.
Nightly till two or three she twirled and span with stately abandon,
bathed in sound. If, as often happened, she found that a young man,
similarly alone, danced closer and closer, and finally with her, that
was fine. If, as happened only slightly less often, the young man decided that a night would be as rewarding as an evening in her company, that was fine too. Her only rule was, never the same one twice.*

One

One of the loneliest sounds in the world is the sound of pacing
heels in an empty room. The larger the room the more desolate
the sound.

We open, then, in the Elgin Marbles room in the British
Museum. The room is empty but for Dr Ann Upnor, lecturer in
Fine Arts at King's College, London. She is pacing the room
slowly from end to end.

Dr Upnor is forty-five. Her most obvious characteristic is a for-
midable chic, a frozen top-to-toe elegance. Whether she is looking
at the Marbles, or simply being in the room, or again simply treating herself to lonely sounds, is open to conjecture. She wears a
very expensive man's wristwatch.

Her pacing has brought her to the middle of the room. She
stops, consults her watch, and is about to sit down when, sensing
someone behind her, she turns sharply round. There is no one.
She sits.

She sits, still, for a long time, until again she senses someone
behind her. She turns round, and sees a figure so grotesque, so
squalid and deformed, that her hand flies to her mouth. Bundled
in rags, its shape twisted, its face a blotch, the figure tries unsuc-
cessfully to speak.

Dr Upnor rummages in, and drops, her bag. Her eyes on the

figure she gropes for her bag, retrieves it, and takes out her purse. She thrusts a pound note at the figure, whose efforts to speak are by now almost frenzied. It gibbers. It pushes the money away. Dr Upnor stands and, handbag open and money still in her hand, flies from the room.

The figure lurches after her, and as she reaches the door manages to utter. Running past Assyrian sculptures Dr Upnor hears four bayed syllables, distorted and amplified by the size of the room and the force of their delivery, but recognizable as her name.

There is a disturbance at the door. Dr Upnor as she walks, her composure regained, through the lunchtime crowd towards the exit sees one of the attendants – William, is it? Yes, William – arguing with a visitor, denying entry. He has stretched out his arm to block the door. Dr Upnor walks up behind him.

What is it, William? she says.

William turns and touches his cap. The person he was trying to keep out slips past him, and darts into the Museum, knocking into Dr Upnor. It is a figure if anything more grotesque than the figure from the Marbles room. Dr Upnor looks after it with horror as it capers crowing away. William shrugs apologetically.

Can't think, he says, what he wants in here. Couldn't even speak properly.

Dr Upnor closes her eyes.

Still, William says. If he wants it that badly.

I must sit down, Dr Upnor says.

Are you all right, doctor? William says. You don't look too good.

That, Dr Upnor says, answers the question then. Doesn't it? Shall we go by appearances for once? I'll be all right if I can sit down.

William fetches a chair and she sits. She is trying hard not to cry.

Would you like some water? William says. I'll get a glass of water.

He goes. Dr Upnor takes a powder compact from her bag and inspects her face.

Jesus Christ! she says.

She dabs her eyes with a handkerchief. William returns with a glass of water, which she drinks.

Thank you, William, she says.

Will I call for a taxi? William says. Really, doctor, you don't look very well.

No, Dr Upnor says. I'll just sit for a while. I'm all right now. My car is just round the corner.

You're sure? William says.

I'll just sit for a while, Dr Upnor says. By myself.

Right then, William says. I'll get back to work.

Yes, Dr Upnor says.

William walks away, and Dr Upnor calls him back.

I'm sorry, William, she says. It was kind of you to bring the water. Thank you.

William nods.

That's all right, he says. My pleasure.

Dr Upnor smiles at him. He looks surprised for a second, then smiles back.

The boy looks worried. Something at the back of Dr Upnor's Rolls-Royce is obviously perplexing him.

Dr Upnor, he says. I'm sorry. I really don't know what to say. Something's happened.

Dr Upnor's manner is not encouraging.

I see, she says. Yes.

Something rather awful, the boy says.

He speaks very quietly.

I don't know how it happened, he says. I can't think.

Perhaps, Dr Upnor says, if you were to tell me what it was. I am rather busy.

You don't recognize me, the boy says.

Quite right, Dr Upnor says. I don't.

I'm Douglas Oblonsky, the boy says.

I see, Dr Upnor says.

I'm one of your students, the boy says.

Yes, Dr Upnor says. So you are. What a day of encounters this is. You sit at the back.

We have met, the boy says. Once.

I remember, Dr Upnor says. At Countess Potocka's. You didn't say much.

I don't, the boy says. Very much. She's my aunt.

A very good reason I expect, Dr Upnor says. Now. Maybe you'd like to tell me what this is about.

Oh, the boy says. Yes. It's rather awkward. My bicycle, you see.

Your bicycle is awkward, Dr Upnor says. I see.

I parked it here, the boy says. I had some work to do. In the library.

Mr Oblonsky, Dr Upnor says, do you want a lift? Is that what you are trying to ask? I did say I was busy.

No, no, the boy says. No. It's not that. Look.

He takes Dr Upnor round to the back of her car and shows her his bicycle. It is chained to her bumper.

I can't get it off, he says.

What on earth? Dr Upnor says. Why on earth did you do it?

I didn't, the boy says. I don't know. It's . . .

It's . . . Dr Upnor says. Indeed it is. Oh really. What an absolutely bloody thing to happen.

I came back, the boy says, and there it was. I don't know what to do.

A man, Dr Upnor says, of decision.

They stand side by side looking at the chained bicycle. Suddenly the absurdity of the situation strikes Dr Upnor and she bursts into laughter. The boy looks at her gravely while she laughs and, eventually, he smiles.

I lied, you know, Dr Upnor says. I'm not busy at all. Day after day with nothing to do. You really don't know?

No, the boy says. I came back and there it was.

You said, Dr Upnor says. Surreal. Well, I suppose we'd better do something about it.

I'm not sure . . . the boy says.

You said that too, Dr Upnor says. There must be somewhere we can telephone. We'll call a garage and they can come and break the chain. We can have some lunch while we wait.

Lunch? the boy says.

Why not? Dr Upnor says. Unless you'd prefer a drink.

No, lunch will do, the boy says. I mean, lunch would be very nice.

Good, Dr Upnor says.

Only, the boy says. Well, you must let me pay.

I wouldn't think of it, Dr Upnor says.

No, I insist, the boy says. I pay. It's my fault, you see.

Mr Oblonsky, Dr Upnor says. You've just spent rather a long time explaining that it isn't.

It is, the boy says. You don't know. I left the bike there. Unlocked. Off the chain. I wanted someone to steal it.

Ah, Dr Upnor says. And that makes it your fault?

Of course, the boy says. I was going to claim on the insurance.

And buying my lunch, Dr Upnor says, will be some sort of expiation. I'm not sure that I want to be your penance.

She smiles. The boy does not.

I see, she says. I am to be the sacrificial lamb. All right. Where's it to be?

There's a place I know, the boy says. Quite near. It's not very grand, I'm afraid.

Well, Dr Upnor says, you're not expiating a very grand dereliction, are you? I'll try to look suitably pained.

Part of the point, the boy says, is that you should enjoy it I expect they have a phone.

A phone? Dr Upnor says.

For the garage, the boy says.

Ah yes, Dr Upnor says. The garage. Shall we go?

She offers her arm to the boy. He, unused to such contact, uneasily takes it.

Her face carefully not dismayed, Dr Upnor follows Douglas into the café and, following his example, takes a tray from the pile at the end of the counter. They move along the counter, Douglas selecting an orange juice and a rum baba. Dr Upnor glances at his choice and takes the same.

I like, she says, rum babas. It's ages since I had one.

It's a sort of baba *au* golden syrup, actually, Douglas says. I think the cream is artificial. And the rum flavour is definitely only flavouring. You get them all over town. I think there must be some sort of central agency, like for the photographs in hairdressers' windows. There are salads and things here. Or if you want something hot the menu's up there.

I think, Dr Upnor says, that's the longest speech you've made yet.

She studies the menu.

It's impossible to tell, she says, how serious you are.

Why should I joke? Douglas says.

Sausage, egg and chips, Dr Upnor says, sound rather nice.

Why, Douglas says, don't you go and phone? I'll see to this. It's over there.

From the phone Dr Upnor sees, as she calls her garage, Douglas order and pay for the food, and find a table next to the window. He carries the trays precariously, one in each hand. Biting in concentration his lower lip, he puts the trays on the table. Dr Upnor finishes her call and stays by the phone to watch as he returns the trays to the counter and goes back to the table. He has, she notices, small feet. He sits with his back to the window. She crosses to the table.

It looks, she says as she sits down, delicious.

Shall we start? he says.

I can't think, she says, of any reason why not.

He bows his head over his food, his hands clasped in his lap. He picks up his orange juice and toasts her.

Cheers, he says.

Cheers, she says.

Well, Dr Upnor says, I thought I was supposed to enjoy this.

Douglas takes care to finish chewing and swallow before he speaks.

I'm sorry, he says. Aren't you? Would you like something else?

The food, she says, is lovely. Of its type. I was beginning to wonder about the conversation. There was a time a few minutes ago when it looked almost as if you were going to say something.

I'm sorry, he says. I'm not good at talking. What would you like me to say?

Whatever, she says, comes into your head. On second thoughts, no. You'd probably relapse into silence. Tell me about yourself.

There isn't . . . he says.

Don't, please, she says, say there isn't much to tell. I don't think I could bear it.

There isn't, he says. I live alone. I have a room.

Do you talk to yourself? she says.

Yes, he says. I do. Why?

So do I, she says. Lonely people do, I notice. Silent in public. Garrulous alone.

I hadn't noticed, he says.

Oh dear, she says. You must be careful or we'll end up talking about me. Why don't we start by finding out why it is you've sat at the back of my lectures for two years without saying anything.

Douglas opens his mouth to speak.

I know, she says. Don't tell me. You don't talk much. You're not a good conversationalist.

How can I say anything, he says, if you talk me down?

Talk louder perhaps, she says. I'm sorry. What were you going to say?

I've sat, he says, at the back of your lectures for eighteen months. I didn't speak because I was too busy listening.

To the cut and thrust, she says, of witty dialogue. Some of them are rather vocal, aren't they?

I was listening, he says, to you.

Ah, she says. A disciple.

A listener, certainly, he says.

We are making, she says, rather heavy weather of this, aren't we?

I was born, Douglas says, in the city of X in the county of Y on a windy afternoon in 1949.

Do you mind if I smoke, Dr Upnor says. This is getting interesting. You don't look that old. Or do you disapprove of smoking between courses?

I don't mind, Douglas says. Go ahead. I'm twenty-two. I was joking.

Why, Dr Upnor says, should you joke?

I thought, Douglas says, that was what you wanted. I thought it was what you were used to. The cut and thrust of witty dialogue. Subtle common-room chit-chat.

So, Dr Upnor says. Let's hide behind Chekhov. You were born in the city of X in the county of Y the son of an infantry officer.

A university lecturer, Douglas says. Another one. In Edinburgh. Medicine.

My father the doctor, Dr Upnor says.

Yes, Douglas says. He died. A long time ago. You wouldn't have liked him. He led a dull life. Good people do, I find.

Dr Upnor looks at him sharply through her cigarette smoke. He is too busy trying to talk to notice.

My grandmother, I think, he says, you would like. If you like Countess Potocka you'd like her. Old world, you see. She left Russia in a dinghy. Rowing out into the gulf of Finland by night. Being shot at by the Reds. All very grand.

I hardly know her, Dr Upnor says. Countess Potocka. She was my husband's friend. I only went there once.

Ah, Douglas says. She's . . .

Look, Dr Upnor says. That's enough. I don't want to talk like this. All this small talk. I don't want it at all. Even though, I suppose, it is what I'm used to. Or would be if it were as witty as you are obviously trying to make it. I want it to stop. All this wit. All this distance. I've been a cow at least three times this morning. You should see me when I'm not trying. The more I think of it, wit

60

is cruelty. More and more clever ways of being cruel. Of diminishing things. I don't know what I want.

Douglas is staring at the table.

Perhaps, he says, that's why I don't make jokes.

Well it's certainly getting interesting now, Dr Upnor says, isn't it? This is hardly the place. Anyway this is supposed to be your expiation, not mine.

Yours is – will be – much grander, Douglas says, of course.

What, Dr Upnor says, a bloody rude thing to say.

Well, isn't it true? Douglas says. If you've got to confess, and God knows why you should, wouldn't you rather do it in – oh, I don't know, Joe Allen's – confessing among the star-spotters? That would be more effective wouldn't it? More valuable?

He takes a deep breath. It is hard to say which appals him more, what he has said, or that he has said it.

It depends, Dr Upnor says, on what you are used to. I'm not used to this.

So much the better, Douglas says.

You think so? Dr Upnor says. I'm not sure. It will seem less real afterwards. It's dangerous to break a habit. It makes everything more immediate, possibly, but much less real. God, how inane I sound! My fluency has deserted me. Another reason why it's dangerous to break a habit.

I don't think it matters too much, Douglas says, about all that. It's all very clever. All very subtle and well-observed. Just as inane in its own way. Does it seem real? Who cares, as long as it is?

He stares again at the table.

I am enormously embarrassed, he says.

What? Dr Upnor says. I didn't hear.

I said, Douglas says, that I was enormously embarrassed.

I told you, Dr Upnor says, we'd end up talking about me.

Douglas looks up and down again.

I can't, he says, think of anyone I'd rather talk about. That was a very stilted compliment. It cost a lot.

Thank you, Dr Upnor says.

You don't understand, Douglas says. Is that the sort of thing your sort of people say all the time? I meant it.

I'm trying, Dr Upnor says. I'm trying to get used to people who mean what they say. I want to start saying what I mean. The main trouble is that it all sounds so dull. But thank you. You see. Little words. Dull.

Because, Douglas says, you haven't understood. Never mind. Thank you will do.

My God! Dr Upnor says. You annoy me, you know that.

She pushes away her sausage, egg and chip-smeared plate.

You sit, she says, at the back of my lectures for eighteen months, in total silence. And then you bring me to a place like this.

I come here quite often, Douglas says.

I don't care, Dr Upnor says, if you come here daily. It's a dump.

Once or twice a week, Douglas says.

Oh come on, Dr Upnor says. Stop behaving like a wounded animal. I want you to come to dinner tonight. I've started my Wednesdays again. Can you come? Seven-thirty for eight.

I should be delighted, Douglas says.

Good, Dr Upnor says.

I'm going to get some coffee, Douglas says. Can I get you some?

While Douglas goes to the counter for coffee, Dr Upnor tackles her rum baba. The cream is artificial.

I didn't know, Douglas says when he gets back, whether you wanted black or white. So I got white.

It's safer, Dr Upnor says.

She sugars her coffee, and offers Douglas the bowl.

I'm going to talk now, she says. So don't interrupt. And it's not going to be easy, because I don't know quite what's wrong. The whole business is very difficult, but it's Wednesday, and Wednesday is truth day. Or my day anyway. I've given dinner parties on Wednesdays for as long as I can remember. Except recently. The last few months. My husband never came to one of them, so I suppose it was silly of me to stop when he died. I'd like to say it was because I didn't feel up to it, but that would be only half true. I don't know why he wouldn't come. He just went out. To begin with I thought he had another woman, so I didn't ask. Then, I suppose, I didn't care. Or didn't notice any more. There was a lot I didn't notice.

Douglas fidgets in his chair.

Be quiet, Dr Upnor says. You'll spoil it. I didn't know what to do with myself when he died. The sheer nakedness of it. Being alone. I had sheltered, you see. Hidden behind him for twenty years. Twenty-odd years. How strange it all is. My first feeling, straight out of the air, when they told me he was dead, was one of pure relief.

She takes a sip of coffee.

I loved him, she says. Always. I never felt anything had really happened to me till I had referred it to him.

The clasp of her watch has come undone. She refastens it.

And the first thing I felt when he died was: now I can go out and have a good time. The very first. I may even have said it aloud. Of course it didn't take me long to realize that that is exactly what loneliness is. Having to go out and have a good time. And then I panicked. One evening, changing to go out, I saw very clearly the sort of woman I was. I stood in front of the mirror and heard a voice in my ear saying, What a cow! What a cow that woman is. She is miserable chicly. A posing bitch. And since then I've tried, approximately, to change. I've tried to teach myself courage. To live immediately. Without reference. But I am the sort of person who hesitates. I consider for two seconds before answering the smallest question. I want to come up with the right answer, and maybe I do, but the hesitation makes it wrong. It's in the family. My husband told me he loved me only once. He didn't have any occasion to tell me again. He would have informed me of any change.

Douglas stands up. His face is scarlet.

Sit down, Dr Upnor says. There's not much more. Can't you cope? The confessing professor. Sit down.

I haven't, you see, Dr Upnor says, felt anything for anyone but myself for years. Even when he died, my first thought was for me.

What I felt for him was not much. And too late. I call our whole life together into question. How can I love the sort of person who can love the sort of person I am?

Practice, Douglas says.

What? Dr Upnor says.

Practice, Douglas says. If he could – if anyone can – so can you.

Dr Upnor says nothing. She touches her watch.

A bit of humility, Douglas says, would help too.

Dr Upnor unfastens and refastens the clasp of her watch.

Maybe, Douglas says, you are not even that big a bitch. I have envied you, you know. In a respectful sort of way. All those months at the back of your class. I've wanted to be like you. So poised. So calm. So certain. I'm not certain of anything.

And now, Dr Upnor says, you see that I'm not either. And I have lost my disciple.

Oh no, Douglas says. No. Quite the reverse.

If Dr Upnor had not been so entirely absorbed in her confession she might have noticed earlier a figure leaning against the window, behind Douglas's chair. Even from behind it is obviously similar to those she saw in the Museum: a stoop, a ragged coat, a filthy stubbled cheek, a crimson cauliflower ear. She sees it now. Rapidly she picks up her bag.

I've got to go, she says. There's someone leaning on the window.

Douglas turns to look.

Oh, he says. Where? Yes. I expect he'll go away.

I think not, Dr Upnor says. I think he's waiting for me. I must go.

She checks her watch.

I've seen him before, she says. Him and the others. For days now. They won't go away. They keep on trying to speak.

She stands.

Look, she says. I must go. Come tonight.

I will, Douglas says. Where to?

Where? Dr Upnor says. Oh yes. 42 Bedford Square.

Seven-thirty for eight, Douglas says.

Dr Upnor leans across the table and kisses him on the cheek.

Thank you for lunch, she says.

Douglas watches her leave the café, and turns to watch her through the window as she hurries up the street. The grotesque figure leaves the window and shambles after her. Douglas turns back to the table and finishes his coffee. This done, he bows his head over the table, as before.

Two

Dom Gervase Plessington OSB, Abbot of Hales, cracks deftly a brazil nut. Brandy circulates and his glass is rarely empty. Conversation is, for the moment, general. Ann, Dom Gervase notes, is touching her watch again, and looking abstracted. There is a burst of laughter, in which Dom Gervase joins. His right-hand neighbour, Sheila Someone-or-other, a spectacularly lovely girl with a fountain of multicoloured hair, has told a joke. The boy is rather pretty too, in a tense, gauche sort of way.

In the silence that follows the laughter Dom Gervase cracks another nut. His shape is as ample as his appetite. He eats hugely. Ann speaks.

What I miss, she says. What I miss most is the shared silence.

The guests look at her in some constraint.

I'm sorry, she says. I wasn't listening.

Dom Gervase helps himself to a pear.

It's all right, my dear, he says. We just didn't expect to be told quite so plainly how unwelcome we were.

Did it sound like that? Ann says. Then I really am sorry. I was thinking. That's all.

The silence continues. The guests shift in their chairs. Dom Gervase bites lusciously into his pear. Sheila laughs.

I'm sorry, she says. But someone has to say something. I for one don't miss silence. I don't need to.

A guest turns to remark to his neighbour.

That's right, Sheila says. Talk among yourselves.

Silence again. Napkins are plied, glasses fingered. Dom Gervase sips his brandy.

Silence, he says, of course . . .

Ah, Sheila says, a Great Thought.

Dom Gervase smiles at her.

Perhaps, he says, you have to be a monk to love silence. It is, we find, the fullest communication. The most evocative utterance.

It can be, Ann says. I don't think it is here. This is an awkward silence.

Or a bored one, Sheila says.

Or a bored one, Ann says. Perhaps that's why you're talking. To avoid boredom.

Or, Dom Gervase says, to encourage silence. Dialogue exists – another Great Thought, I'm afraid – to put silence into context.

It's a question, Sheila says, of the lesser of two evils. The dullness of silent communion, or aimless conversation.

Parties, of course, Dom Gervase says, are enforced dialogue.

How well we are doing, Sheila says. The others are hanging on our every word. They at least don't love silence. They are not like us. They don't see its possibilities.

You don't seem too at home in it yourself, Ann says. It was you who complained of boredom.

Up the table, two guests put their heads together.

Oh dear, Sheila says. I've lost my audience.

One of the speakers, without turning his head, gives a V-sign under his arm, and carries on talking.

An example of silent communion, Ann says. End of phase one, Sheila, I think. Collapse of first bid for dominance.

Sheila and Dom Gervase exchange glances. Conversation becomes general again.

I've been seen through, Sheila says.

Well, Dom Gervase says, it makes things easier, doesn't it? I suppose it's an obvious question, but if you dislike Ann so much, why do you come to her party?

Oh, Sheila says, anything for a free meal, you know. I have taken no vow of austerity.

Dom Gervase replenishes his glass.

Is that, Sheila says, another example of a speaking silence? I suppose it must be. Oh please, don't smile again. It gives me a pain.

That, Dom Gervase says, and what else?

Oh no, Sheila says. You can't slot me that easily. I'm in pain so I hit out. How penetrating. How wise.

I wish, Dom Gervase says, I could say, Never mind. It will be over soon. Just keep on taking the pills.

Oh doctor, doctor, Sheila says. I get these dreadful pains. You make me sick, you know that? You and she. All these people who know what they want.

Is that what we seem, Dom Gervase says. I wonder. I hope so, of course. We teach by precept. To all intents and purposes we are what we seem.

I wouldn't like to say, Sheila says, how you seem to me.

You don't have to, Dom Gervase says. Your silence speaks.

I don't believe it, Sheila says. You've done it again. You have me in the corner again.

It's where you want to be, Dom Gervase says. So there's no skill in it.

If you don't mind, Sheila says, I think I'll be quiet for a while. *Pour mieux sauter.* The end of my second bid for dominance. I must look to my laurels.

She turns away.

Dom Gervase eats.

Ann, he observes, though talking to her neighbour, is looking at the boy. The boy has said, as far as Dom Gervase can remember, nothing all evening. He sits quietly over his far from empty glass. As Dom Gervase watches, he looks up and catches Ann's eye. She smiles at him and he looks away again. Dom Gervase frowns.

Ann, he says. You don't look well.

Ann stops what she is saying and looks at Dom Gervase in surprise.

67

The evening is a strain, of course, Dom Gervase says. Under the circumstances.

Gervase, Ann says. What on earth are you talking about? I'm fine.

Dom Gervase looks at the boy. Ann follows his eyes. Sheila watches closely.

I shouldn't care, he says, to see you out of your depth. There is no substitute for grief. The difficulty is to recover unscathed. To cherish the loss. Not to regret it, or fly from it, or bury it. To do that is to cheat yourself.

Ann touches her watch.

I don't think, she says, that this is the time or the place. Everyone has stopped talking again. I can look after my own recovery, Gervase.

Dom Gervase is about to speak but Sheila forestalls him.

Not another *bon mot*, please, she says. I couldn't stand another conversation on the nature of silence.

You showed every sign, Ann says, of enjoying the last one. Or most of it.

Our opinions, Sheila says, like our emotions are ephemeral.

She looks at the boy.

There now, she says. I have made a *bon mot*. I didn't think I had it in me.

Sheila, Ann says, would you mind bouncing back a bit later. I don't feel up to you quite yet.

Sheila waves her hand towards Dom Gervase.

If, she says, you can defend yourself against his insinuations, you can defend yourself against mine. The semblance of bereft fragility will do as well in either case, surely?

She addresses the whole table.

This is my last party, you see, she says. I intend to go out with a bang.

You don't know me, Ann says, or my parties, if you think your rudeness will get you banned. Come again. Any time.

Oh God! Sheila says. Not another one. I haven't got myself involved in some ghastly sort of group therapy, have I? Have I found another great healer? Oh well, it's in the family, I suppose.

Ann does not understand and, for a moment before she turns away, shows it. Sheila, flushed and breathless with daring, sits back in her chair. The boy, at last, sips his brandy.

You did quite well there, Dom Gervase says. You have sown a doubt.

Good, wasn't it, Sheila says. I told you I was just drawing breath.

I suppose, Dom Gervase says, you will choose your own moment to explain. You weren't Geoffrey's mistress, were you?

Sheila laughs.

What a delicious word, she says. I don't think I've ever heard it used outside books.

How old-fashioned I am, Dom Gervase says. I am one of those trying people who pre-empt criticism by admitting the grounds. Were you? His mistress, or lover, or what you will?

I must sit at your feet, Sheila says. I have so much to learn.

Well, Dom Gervase says. Teachers are necessary. Were you?

Oh come! Sheila says. You can do better than that. You sound as if you were entering for truism of the year.

Come to that, Dom Gervase said, I don't think I've ever heard anyone say, Oh come! before. The important thing about a truism, of course, is that it's true. Oh dear, another *bon mot*.

Sheila presses her temples and closes her eyes.

God, she says. I'm tired.

Ah, Dom Gervase says. The human touch. I was waiting for it.

Sheila stretches for the brandy bottle and pours herself a large glass. She offers the bottle to Dom Gervase, who helps himself as liberally.

I think, Sheila says, I shall get even drunker.

I think, Dom Gervase says, I shall join you. This is going to be a bumpy night.

Sheila stares at him in sheer surprise. They both roar with laughter.

There is, of course, general silence again, except for the cascades of laughter.

Whatever, Ann says as they gradually subside, is so funny?

Nothing, Dom Gervase says. Really. Nothing at all.

We were talking, Sheila says. What were we talking about?

Teaching, Dom Gervase says. We decided it was necessary.

Ann's mouth is trembling. She covers it with her hand.

Yes, she says. Well. It is. I think. I hope. I don't suppose anyone devotes his life to anything really, but you and I together, Gervase, have been teaching for over seventy years.

And you suppose, Dom Gervase says, that we haven't lived our life in vain. And how are we to know whether we have or not? We could very easily be wrong.

And if you are, Sheila says.

How should I know, Dom Gervase says. All that matters is resignation. The Will of God is a joy to those that love him. We are taught to suffer injustice gladly.

Reference, Ann says, is what matters. Continual reference to other people.

For the first time the boy sustains her regard without turning away.

There was once, Ann says, a great violinist.

The guests settle in their chairs. It is story time. Dr Upnor's Wednesdays, like her lectures, are famous for their stories. Sheila's hands, Dom Gervase sees, are gripped tight together in her lap.

His speciality, Ann says, was the works of Bach. He played them all over the world, and no two performances were the same. With each playing he discovered new felicities, different nuances, different angles from which to look at the whole.

On his way to a concert tour of Australia, the boat on which he was travelling went down in mid-ocean, and he was marooned, as far as he knew the only survivor, on an island. He had managed to save his violin and, as he was alone on his island for some months, he used the time to practise and perfect his art. He decided to concentrate on one work and master the definitive performance. He had no music with him, so he chose the piece he knew best, the second suite, and played it constantly, each day discovering new resonances, until he had explored it fully. Then, using the knowledge he had gained from that work, he moved on to others, each time extracting the true essence of the work.

Time passed and he was rescued, and on the boat that rescued him was his agent, who was delighted to hear that the master had discovered in his solitude the one true way of playing Bach, and arranged an enormous concert to publicize this revolutionary breakthrough. The concert was held in New York, and music lovers from all over the world gathered to hear it.

It was a total failure. Within minutes the distinguished audience was coughing and twisting in its seat, and before the end of the first piece the concert dissolved in laughter. The music, as one critic said, was unrecognizable either as Bach or indeed as music. The performer, during his long exile, had lost contact with humanity. Without the verification of human contact, his discoveries had no meaning.

Tears flow down Ann's cheeks. She rests her head in her hands.

Sheila ungrips her hands and claps.

Well done, she says. Bravo. Is it finished?

She looks around the table.

And who can tell me, she says, where that little parable gets us?

I didn't, Ann says, really expect you to see. To the blind ugliness cannot exist. It presupposes a sense they do not possess. But then I wasn't really talking to you.

Not even your teaching, Sheila says, can do me any good, is that it? Only the chosen get the treatment. So what's the good of all this conscience-stricken vaporizing if it can't comprise everybody, even me? My God, Dr Upnor! What a wanker you are.

I can't find it in me, Ann says, to be annoyed. I know I ought to but I can't. I just don't think your opinions are worth a pin.

And I, Sheila says, am waiting for proof that yours are more valuable.

I think, Dom Gervase says, we will stop this conversation now. I see no reason why we should all continue to be distressed by some private peevishness. I think you should go now.

I'll go, Sheila says, when I'm good and ready. I'm not ready yet. I haven't got what I came for yet. I've been waiting all evening for some truth. For some construction. Some honest destruction would have been acceptable too. But all I've found is oh-so-gentle restraint. Oh-so-self-conscious resignation. Let's make it quite plain that we're suffering, and make a show of how stoically we bear it. Shall I tell you how she's been bearing it? Out every night of the week. Whoring. Every night a new . . . escort, is that the word? Well, is it?

Ann sits absolutely still. Dom Gervase dissects a peach.

No answer, Sheila says. No answer for Sheila. Well, escort will do. God knows, I have no objection to a good fuck.

Broad-minded of you, Dom Gervase says.

Isn't it? Sheila says. Nothing more soothing than a good fuck. But be honest about it. Admit it. She even has the latest one sitting here with us, and she's not going to admit it. Why doesn't she tell us what she's learned?

I can tell you about it, Dom Gervase says, if you want to know. Do you want to know, or just to embarrass us?

Both, I think, Sheila says. To embarrass her certainly.

Well then, Dom Gervase says.

Oh God! Sheila says. I can hear it all already. We've had it all before. Grief and dignity. Sin and repentance. What do you know about it? What do you know about waking up in the middle of the night not knowing whose is the body next to you?

Perhaps, Dom Gervase says, more than you think. I can tell you, too, about the sheer muscular relief when that body gets out of bed in the morning. I can tell you about post-orgasmic depression, and pre-orgasmic depression, and hideous breakfasts with total strangers. I can tell you all about one-night stands. At least as much as you can tell me. I can tell you how exactly they demonstrate the impenetrability of solitude.

Words, Sheila says. Just long words. Why must you always

generalize everything? Conceptualize everything. We were talking about her.

We were talking, Dom Gervase says, about you, surely? At least, I was.

Deflected again, Sheila says. How casually! With what grace! Well, now I am going. One thing I can tell you. One spark of honesty before I go. I can tell you where the late lamented Geoffrey Upnor spent his Wednesdays. No, it's all right. He wasn't with me. You can breathe again. You'll never believe it. He was in Beckenham. He was a faith healer.

She stands up. Ann looks at the boy.

Help me, she says.

The boy says nothing.

All right, Sheila says. Don't listen. I'll tell everyone else.

She kicks back her chair and walks round the table to the door.

A Messiah, she says. Every Wednesday. Off to some lunatic woman's cripple asylum in Beckenham. Laying on his hands in Beckenham. Spreading the word in Beckenham. I ask you. How bourgeois can you get? A Messiah on Wednesdays. She turns on Dom Gervase.

I think, she says, that beats even you.

There is silence at the table as Sheila leaves. Her walk across the hall and the slam of the front door are the only things to break the silence.

What an exit! Dom Gervase says. Not a good thinker. But a fine actress. Ann, you must lay her on again.

They laugh. Even the boy manages a smile. Dom Gervase lifts Sheila's scarf from where she has left it over the back of her chair.

Poor Sheila, Ann says. However will she get it back?

Ann can only keep up appearances with a visible effort. There is a loud knocking at the door. The boy gets up.

No, Ann says. I'll go. It will be Sheila back for her scarf. I wonder how she'll carry it off.

The boy sits, and Ann leaves to open the door. After a while, the boy takes Sheila's scarf and leaves too. The knocking is heard again. And again. The front door is heard to slam.

When it becomes obvious that neither Ann nor the boy is going to return, smiles circulate among the guests. Dom Gervase pours himself a brandy. Gradually the guests disperse. When they have all gone Dom Gervase pushes away his plate, drains his glass, and sits, waiting.

Three

On her way from the dining room to the front door, Dr Upnor pauses in front of the hall mirror, and leans her forehead on the glass.

Cool, she says. Cool. Cool.

The knocking on the door is repeated, and Dr Upnor stands up straight. There is a mark left by her forehead on the mirror. She rubs it with her hand, which leaves a worse smear than ever. She bunches her skirt and makes to wipe the mirror with it, but the knocking on the door prevents her and, with an impatient intake of breath, she goes to open it.

It is not Sheila. It is a fourth, or possibly the same for the fourth time, grotesque figure. Dr Upnor gags and with all her force slams the door. Turning from the door she sees Douglas standing in the middle of the hall. She goes to him and puts her arms around him, crying. For a while Douglas doesn't move his arms from his side. Then he pats her gently on the back.

I can stop it, he says. All this.

Gradually Dr Upnor stops crying. She releases Douglas and goes to the mirror.

If you come with me, Douglas says. I can stop it. You needn't see any of them again.

I should like, Dr Upnor says, to rest for a while.

Well, Douglas says. Shall we go then?

Dr Upnor turns from the mirror.

Let's go, she says.

She points to the dining-room door.

They can look after themselves, she says.

74

I don't think I can promise a rest, Douglas says. Not yet.

Oh well, Dr Upnor says. A change then. Where shall we go?

I'll drive, Douglas says.

Gervase is right, of course, Dr Upnor says. I have lost my sense of sin. What is life without a sense of sin?

She is lying back in her seat while Douglas drives. Her eyes are closed.

We live, she says, in a world of immediate gratification. What I want I can have. But then, because I have it, I can't keep it.

Douglas drives in silence.

He reminds me, Dr Upnor says, of Giant Despair. Gervase. Give up everything. Always saying, Give up everything. We only keep what we give up. Of course it hurts. That's why we keep it. The loss and the pain make us keep it.

She opens her eyes.

Where are we? she says.

Driving, Douglas says.

There has to be a way, she says. Hasn't there? There must be a way of being happy that doesn't involve giving things up. I won't believe that the only way to get peace in the world is to ignore it. Sheila was right. All this self-conscious resignation. But we are self-conscious. We all have to be self-conscious. There is nothing else to be conscious of. A life sentence in the dungeon of the self.

Phrases, Douglas says. Phrase maker.

A wanker, Dr Upnor says.

Yes, if you like, Douglas says. A wanker. The search for truth is not a search for accuracy. Ending up in a phrase. Oh, an accurate phrase. A telling phrase. Yes, and a truthful phrase. A life sentence in the dungeon of the self. Very good. But a wank all the same. Its accuracy is soothing. Its truthfulness is beautiful, and therefore healing, and therefore inaccurate. Anaesthetizing with beauty the horror of the fact.

I'm tired, Dr Upnor says. Where are we going?

I'm not surprised, Douglas says. Those were not nice people. Not good people. Not right.

My sort of people, Dr Upnor says. I'm afraid.

Above all, Douglas says, not that. Not your sort of people. They are the wrong sort of cripple. The dangerous kind. They want everyone else to be crippled too. The jealous kind. They have no joy. Not even in other people's lack of their pain.

That sounds like a good description of me, Dr Upnor says.

Douglas accelerates.

All right, Dr Upnor says. I didn't mean it. All right. Not my sort of people.

Douglas slows down again.

Though why, Dr Upnor says, you think you can see more clearly than I can, I can't think.

Douglas drives in silence.

Why you force me to pretend, Dr Upnor says, you know me better than I know myself, I can't think.

She closes her eyes again.

I love you, Douglas says. Sometimes the thought of you stops me dead in the street.

Where are we going? Dr Upnor says.

The house is large and tumbledown. The headlights pick out an overgrown garden and an almost collapsed porch. Douglas leads Dr Upnor by a puddled path to the back door.

The kitchen is not clean, and full of heterogeneous furniture. On the table and in the sink are the remains of a meal, a congealing joint of lamb, a tub of well-turned mashed potato, and shreds of cabbage in a colander.

The drawing room is huge and stuffed with every kind of chair. A candle burns before a stand of icons in a corner. A tall grey-haired woman is playing a piano, and around the room sits a crowd of people as odd and as various as the chairs they sit on, among them the grotesque figures, now revealed as separate, that have been pursuing her.

Dr Upnor looks around the room and her mouth twitches. She goes back into the kitchen.

She sits at the kitchen table. Douglas comes back from the drawing room, closes the connecting door, and stands by her chair.

What is this place? Dr Upnor says.

Home, Douglas says. It's where I live.

And those people, Dr Upnor says. In there.

Friends, Douglas says. Friends of Galina's. This is her house.

They live here too? Dr Upnor says.

Some of them, Douglas says. There are a lot of rooms upstairs. And we built some huts in the garden. Most of them are visitors. They come every Wednesday.

Everything, Dr Upnor says, is so . . .

She hesitates.

Dirty is the word you're looking for, Douglas says. Damp too. We don't have much money. Galina is my guardian.

And these people, Dr Upnor says, are friends of yours.

I know most of them, Douglas says.

So, Dr Upnor says. It was a plan.

A plan of Galina's, Douglas says. I haven't said a word that wasn't true.

Galina, Dr Upnor says. I suppose I shall see her soon.

She'll be out, Douglas says.

He sits next to her.

She's playing the piano, he says.

Then I suppose, Dr Upnor says, we wait.

Dr Upnor, Douglas says. This is my guardian. Baroness Galina von Nolde.

Galina is in her sixties, and appallingly dressed. She wears a grey workman's shirt, a full-length wraparound floral skirt, and coarse sandals revealing dirty feet. She is tall and stately. Her face is seamed and tranquil, her grey hair drawn back into a bun. Her dirty hands are clasped in front of her. She walks with balletic poise.

I am glad to meet you, Baroness, Dr Upnor says.

Galina Sergeievna, Galina says. You can't be as glad to see us as we are to see you. We have been expecting you for some time.

I'm flattered, Dr Upnor says. You have gone to some trouble to find me.

To fetch you, Galina says. We have always known where you were.

Yes, Dr Upnor says. I suppose you have Mr Oblonsky to thank for that.

Not at all, Galina says. Douglas is a Count, you know.

I didn't, Dr Upnor says. I'm sorry. Little bastard.

Shall we go through, Galina says. To my room.

I want to go home, Dr Upnor says. I just thought I'd mention it. I don't want to be here at all.

Galina moves to the connecting door.

My room, she says, is through here.

I could drive away now, Dr Upnor says. I don't suppose the Count has let down my tyres. Or taken off the distributor head.

Douglas, still sitting at the table, hands her the car keys. She takes them and stands up.

Galina opens the connecting door. Dr Upnor pockets her keys and walks through into the drawing room. Galina follows her.

Douglas does not move.

Galina claps her hands.

Dr Upnor is standing in the middle of the room.

The occupants pay no attention to either of them. Some are playing cards. Some knit. Some merely sit.

It is Wednesday, Galina says. Dr Upnor is back.

There is no reaction. Someone hums, a long continuous noise. Dr Upnor looks around, expectant. Suddenly, behind her, an old woman bursts into song:

Sweet the moments, rich in blessing
Which before the cross I spend.

Dr Upnor turns and the singer takes her by the hand, gazing earn-estly into space. She sings and sings. Dr Upnor fights down a desire to laugh, and looks for help to Galina, who gives no sign.

Gently at first, then firmly, Dr Upnor disengages her hand. The woman sings on without pause. Galina moves to an inner door, and shows Dr Upnor into a dark corridor.

Dr Upnor leans against the wall and laughs.

I'm sorry, she says. I can't help it.

That was Irena, Galina says. She's quite dotty.

I'm sorry, Dr Upnor says. I shall stop soon. There. Oh dear. I'm sorry.

Yes, Galina says. This way.

Galina's room, too, is stuffed with furniture, some of it boarding-house lumpy, some of it gilt and grand and very beautiful. The walls are papered with innumerable photographs. By the window is painter's clutter and an easel holding a picture of striking chastity, three bottles on a grey ground. Dr Upnor is immediately absorbed by the picture.

Galina goes to a cupboard and produces a battered tray, a mug, a priceless glass and a matching decanter. She sets the tray on a low table by her chair, a high-backed dining chair, on which she sits bolt upright.

This, Dr Upnor says, is very, very beautiful. Did you paint it?

Yes, Galina says. It's just finished.

So I see, Dr Upnor says. It is very good. May I buy it?

No, Galina says. It is not for sale.

I'm sorry, Dr Upnor says.

Not at all, Galina says. Do sit down. Would you like some plum wine? We make it ourselves.

Dr Upnor sits in an armchair.

Of course, she says.

Galina pours plum wine into the glass and the mug, and gestures that Dr Upnor should take one. Dr Upnor hesitates between the mug and the glass, finally selecting the glass. Galina, unaware as far as Dr Upnor can see, of any difference, takes the mug. Dr Upnor shifts in her chair.

May I move? she says. I'm afraid this chair is damp.

She moves to the next chair.

Better? Galina says.

Not really, Dr Upnor says.

You mustn't mind them, Galina says. Sometimes they give us a little trouble, but they'll be all right now you're here. Don't expect them to pay you much attention. You are necessary to them and they resent that. You are a fact of life, like the floor they walk on. Too necessary to talk to, even if they could manage to talk, which many of them can't. But they feel, when they feel, that they have as much to give you as you can give them. We helped them, your husband and I, but we used them too. Does that make sense to you yet?

Why did you say, Dr Upnor says, Dr Upnor is back?

He was Dr Upnor too, Galina says. They make little distinction between skirts and trousers. And none at all between History and Fine Arts. Your husband had it all, you know. He talked to them about history. He wrote his books in there. In that room. They didn't hear a word. They loved him immensely. They were desolated when he stopped coming. We had a lot of trouble. Incidents. So I told them about you. I sent them out to find you. They will be very glad you've come.

Dr Upnor sips her plum wine and puts it aside.

What on earth, she says, can I do? I wouldn't have any idea, the first idea, what to do.

There is no need, Galina says, to do anything much. Talk, smile, touch every now and again. It is more important to be than to do. You could lavish help and love on them and if you were not yourself they would spit it back at you. I have a job for you.

A job, Dr Upnor says. I haven't decided to stay yet.

One must not decide, Galina says. One must do. You won't decide to stay. You will stay.

You are very sure of me, Dr Upnor says.

Dr Upnor, Galina says, you are a typical teacher. You mask your failure under a cloak of scholarship. How long is it now since you felt a spark of sympathy? A year? Two years? Four? We are going to change all that.

You have a job for me, Dr Upnor says.

Upstairs, Galina says. Two floors up. An old woman is dying. She was a servant all her life. She is at home in attics. She is dying, believe me, most ungracefully, in filth and stink and a certain joy. You must help her. Don't be afraid. You will be disgusted and distressed. It is most important that this does not show. You need not pity her. She lived joyfully, lovingly in the face of death. Death by now is her old friend. She is almost a hundred years old. She needs you.

Why? Dr Upnor says. If death is such an old friend, why does she need me?

You're not drinking your wine, Galina says. Don't you like it?

Imagine you are a child, Galina says. You are going to visit a friend. You are going to spend the summer in Provence with a dear friend from school. You are looking forward to it. But when the day comes for you to leave and the cab is at the door, everyone has gone out, on business, visiting, shopping. There is no one to say goodbye to. Are you happy? You are off to have a lovely time. Are you happy?

I see, Dr Upnor says. What shall I say to her?

You don't listen, Galina says. Whatever you say she won't hear. She is deaf. She can't move. She can only just think. What does it matter what you say?

So why, Dr Upnor says, does it have to be me?

I told you, Galina says. They feel they have as much to give you as you them. How can you fight if you don't listen?

Maybe, Dr Upnor says, I can't hear either.

Maybe, Galina says. This is your test. To see if you are as good as they. What is there about you that is special? They know, those lunatics in there. And you do not. You must learn the faculty of trust. You have been hurt. Heal yourself. Trust the knife as it stabs you. Don't your religious friends tell you that? If you believe that love is important, then you must love. Irrespective. In spite of, because of, loss, hurt, betrayal. How else?

Thank you, Dr Upnor says, for the sermon. Just this once, though. To set me on my way. Tell me what to say.

You will stay then? Galina says.

I am here, Dr Upnor says. I will speak to your friend. I can't promise any more.

Good, Galina says. You are learning. Promises are evil. They presuppose a lack of trust.

Dr Upnor stands up. She is very stiff. She brushes her clothes.

Just as damp as the other, I'm afraid, Galina says.

Yes, Dr Upnor says.

Follow me, Galina says.

On the table by the bed is a photograph of a young man in uniform, a china spittoon, and a glass containing water and an artificial eye. The smell is vile. Dr Upnor stands back behind the door and retches violently. Her eyes water. She takes a deep breath and re-enters the room. Galina is sitting on the bed. She takes the old woman's hand. There are icons again in the corner of the room.

Dr Upnor est arrivée, ma petite, Galina says. *Elle est venue vous dire bon voyage.*

Dr Upnor takes Galina's place on the bed. Galina leaves and closes the door. The old woman appears to be asleep. Dr Upnor takes her hand.

Um, she says.

She looks around the room. There is the bed, a table, a chair, and a chest of drawers. And the icons.

What in the name of God, Dr Upnor says, am I doing here? That little bastard.

She lays down the old woman's hand and goes to inspect the icons.

From a purely professional point of view, she says, very poor quality. Prints, my God. Windows into Heaven.

She goes to the window and tries to open it. It is stuck.

Windows into Heaven, she says. And the eyes are windows into the soul.

She looks back to the bed. The old woman's one eye is open. Dr Upnor manages a glassy smile. The old woman's eye continues to stare. Dr Upnor's smile thins and dies, and she looks out of the window. Then she laughs and goes to sit on the bed.

I've come to say good-bye, she says. They told me you don't hear. You don't understand a thing. Anyway, I suppose I should be speaking French. She did. I don't know how long I'm supposed to stay. I hate good-byes. Prolonged good-byes. Tear-stained handkerchiefs. Waving till your arm aches. Quite unnecessary. Good-bye. Good-bye. That's all you need. The more you love someone the less there is to say. The harder it is to say it.

She takes the old woman's hand.

I am not a good actress, she says. At least not now. Socially I can act. I can smooth over most things. Keep it smooth. But how can anyone smooth this? Anyway, I'm not supposed to act. Just to be. To be me. God knows what comfort there can be in that. But it's yours, whatever it is. Take it. May it make you happy.

With her other hand she touches the old woman's hair.

One should never forget, she says, as I've been telling myself, over and over again for weeks now, how very strange it is to go to bed with a total stranger. Well, I can manage that well enough. I thought that's what I was going to be doing this very evening. Right now. Or maybe it would have been over by now. You lose track of time. But I could have done it easily, and it's no less strange than this. Loving a total stranger.

The old woman's eye closes and starts open again.

I can't love you, Dr Upnor says. It's silly to pretend. It's silly to try. But I can be here, if you like. I can face it. All this. Outstare it. Survive it. Intact. Nothing a good bath won't cure.

The old woman coughs enormously. The bed shakes. She dribbles and hawks. Dr Upnor grabs the spittoon and holds it to her mouth.

So, Dr Upnor says. I have found my vocation. A Messiah on Wednesdays. Ann Psychopompos, the leader of souls. Compound nouns have no gender. I want to go home. I want to go to bed.

The old woman speaks. Dr Upnor does not hear. She looks

at her watch. It is ten past twelve. The old woman speaks again.

I can't hear, Dr Upnor says.

With a startling clarity the old woman speaks again.

Où est mon oeil, she says.

Dr Upnor laughs.

Your eye? She says. Where is your eye?

Où est mon oeil, the old woman says.

Dr Upnor sees the artificial eye in the glass.

Ah, she says.

She fishes the eye out of the glass and puts it into the old woman's hand. The hand closes convulsively on the eye.

Mon oeil, the old woman says.

Dr Upnor lifts her head and smooths her pillow. Slowly the old woman smiles. It is some time before Dr Upnor realizes that she is smiling at her. She tries to smile back but finds that she cannot. She takes off her watch and leaves it on the table. She bends over the old woman and kisses her on the forehead.

Bon voyage, she says.

You can hear the noise from the stairs. Dr Upnor, her face washed and freshly made up, Douglas passed unacknowledged, maybe unseen, in an upper corridor, opens the drawing-room door. Hoots, yells and screams come from within. Galina, her finger marking her place in a book, stands at the piano, the one still point in the room. Hands clap. Feet stamp. Above the noise rises the sound of Irena's hymn.

Dr Upnor pushes her way with difficulty through the crowd. Hands pluck and clutch at her as she passes. She reaches Galina at the piano. They have to shout to make themselves heard.

They want, Galina says, you to talk to them.

One isn't enough? Dr Upnor says.

Once a week, Galina says. Every Wednesday.

She hands Dr Upnor the book.

This is what I was using, she says. It will do for today. They are not good with substitutes. Remember.

She leaves.

Dr Upnor opens the book at random and reads. At first she is inaudible, but gradually the noise subsides and she can be heard. She is reading from *Pride and Prejudice*.

The occupants of the room have returned to their former activities. They play cards. They knit. They sit. They talk to themselves. They do not listen.

Dr Upnor is absorbed in her reading. She does not notice Douglas when he comes in and sits at the back of room. He sits and watches her, and quietly slips out again.

Now we are outside Galina's house, waiting by Dr Upnor's car. It is about half past two. The house is dark but for an upper window. Soon Douglas's silhouette appears at the window and we hear the sound of footsteps approaching over muddy gravel. Galina is seeing Dr Upnor to her car.

Next week, Dr Upnor is saying, I'll bring some slides. I'll give a lecture. I'm working out something really interesting on Vermeer. It should be ready by then.

Wait here, Galina says.

She goes back into the house. Dr Upnor looks out across the lawn to the patch of light thrown by Douglas's window. The front door of the house opens and Galina comes out carrying her picture.

For you, she says.

A reward? Dr Upnor says.

Certainly not, Galina says. A present.

Thank you, Dr Upnor says. I shall treasure it.

Hang it, Galina says. Look at it from time to time. That's what it's for. It's not a treasure.

Dr Upnor opens the car door and carefully puts the picture on the passenger seat. She gets into the car, closes the door and winds down the window.

She's dead, you know, Galina says. She died while you were reading.

Ah, Dr Upnor says.

She starts the car.

Poor Douglas, Galina says.

Little bastard, Dr Upnor says. Say good-bye to him from me.

Good-bye? Galina says.

Yes, Dr Upnor says. I think so. Until next week, Baroness.

She winds up the window. Galina goes back into the house. Maybe, as she backs and turns the car, Dr Upnor sees Douglas's silhouette immobile at his window. She certainly does not look.

HIDING

Willy Graham was sitting on the window-seat, conscious of the fat plush feel of buttoned velvet against his short-trousered thighs. He squirmed.

Mummy, he said.

Mm? his mother said.

Willy watched with fascination as his mother carefully smoothed redness on to her arched upper lip, then pressed her lips together and wiped the corners with a tissue.

Mummy, he said.

Mm? his mother said, leaning forward to inspect the result of her labour, adjusting the side mirror the better to catch her profile.

Mummy, Willy said.

His mother palpated cream into her throat.

Mm? she said.

Mummy, Willy said.

QX, QX, QX, his mother said to the mirror, exaggerating the motions of the sound, and feeling the tendons of her throat.

Mummy, Willy said.

His mother turned on her seat to face him.

Yes? she said. Yes? What?

Willy, who had wanted to smile, and his mother to smile, so that they could share a smile, said: Nothing. He squirmed again on the window-seat. The plump velvet crept under his thighs.

Willy's mother turned back to her make-up. Willy, who loved to brush his mother's hair, and often climbed into her bed when his father had left it, and woke her with gentle brush-strokes, watched her pick up her brush, but judged the moment inopportune to ask, his mother's temper, uncertain at the best of times, too uncertain. It was never safe to take his mother's reactions for granted. A month ago she had bought him a nightlight. They had made a game of setting it, a stubby candle wrapped in greased paper, in a saucer of water. Lighting it was a nightly ritual for a week, till one night she forgot. Willy lit it himself. When it ran out a few days later, and Willy asked for another, he was answered with a gulp, a Willy will you never grow up, and a flood of tears.

Well, Willy's mother said. That's finished.

She turned and smiled at Willy.

Come on, she said. We'll be late. I expect Daddy's waiting.

Where are we going? Willy said.

Come and give me a kiss, his mother said.

Willy climbed down from the window-seat and crossed to his mother. She bent and kissed his forehead.

What a dirty nose, she said. Use one of these.

Willy blew his nose on the proffered tissue. His mother stood up.

What a noddle, she said.

Willy folded the tissue and put it in his trouser pocket. His mother went to the wardrobe and selected a hat. As he watched her pick up this hat and that and finally settle on a pill-box and veil, his hand sneaked the lipstick from the dressing table and put it in his pocket along with the tissue.

Come on, Willy, his mother said. I told you. Daddy's waiting.

Willy caught sight of himself in the mirror, a smear of lipstick on his forehead from his mother's kiss. Back from the wardrobe his mother swooped, and scooped him on to the dressing stool, his face level with hers. She wiped his forehead and set him on the floor again.

What a noddle, she said, and went to the door saying, Come on.

Willy turned to the mirror and saluted himself, naval fashion.

Roger, he said. Coming on now.

Reflected in the mirror his mother laughed. She raised an imaginary pipe to her lips and whistled. Willy turned about and marched to the door. His mother raised the pitch of her whistle as he passed her and piped him out of her bedroom. From the corner of his eye Willy noticed for the first time the gross swag of her belly. He was engulfed in embarrassment. Sweating he kept up his quick march to the stair head, repeating inwardly, God she's so fat, she's so fat, my God she's so fat. By the time he was half-way down the stairs the chant was just words and his embarrassment passed.

Captain Graham, Royal Navy retired, now a farmer, looked up from his post at the hall door.

Hello sailor, he said.

Where are we going, Willy said.

Sherborne, his father said.

Diddle's place? Willy said.

Diddle's place, his mother said as she followed him down the stairs, makes it sound like the corner of a field. Whatever else it is, it's not that.

Yes, his father said, Diddle's place.

Diddle was Willy's cousin, and had been his best friend. Till Willy went away to school they had seen each other almost every day. Diddle's father was Willy's father's brother, and business partner, and had been his best friend. Till Diddle's father moved to Sherborne they had seen each other every day. Willy's mother decided to have Willy, and Diddle's mother decided to have Diddle, on the same day. The fact that Willy took ten months longer to arrive was, as Willy's mother said, no fault of hers. The two boys grew up together. They bruised their ankles together on summer picnics in stubble fields. They fell together into the same puddles and tore their trousers on the same fences. The two families went on holiday together: two weeks every year, after the harvest, in a rented bungalow on the sea front at Dymchurch. When they spent the night at each other's house, as they did two or three times a week, the two boys shared the same bed.

Then Willy went away to school, and when he came home after his first term, Diddle's father had moved. Commerce between the two families dwindled. When Willy and Diddle were in the room conversation was stilted and obstructed by long silences. Goodbyes were strained. Diaries were consulted when future meetings were mentioned.

Diddle too seemed different: older and less accessible. He wore jeans. He smoked, swore, and was less inclined to play games. Nowadays he preferred fights, which he always won, and competitions, like who could jump higher, and further, and more dangerously, from the swing rope in the barn, and became bad-tempered if he lost. He didn't listen any more to Willy's stories. Where before he had sat in spellbound silence in their special hiding place as Willy retold *Pilgrim's Progress*, *Gulliver's Travels*, or *Wuthering Heights*, now he yawned, and slapped Willy's shoulder, and turned away. Willy tried to tell him about school, a terrible place, a place which gave him bad dreams, but Diddle just laughed, and called him wet, and pushed him into a pile of straw. Sometimes he threw himself on top of Willy. Sometimes he sat on his head. Sometimes, half-way through a fight, he would insist that they took off all their clothes before they carried on. Once he startled Willy very much by asking if he could pee on his back, and was so put out by Willy's refusal that he didn't speak till tea-time. He asked other things too, which Willy did not refuse, but couldn't see the point of. It was all, Willy felt, confusing, and not very nice, and probably not worth the long car journey.

Diddle's place, he said. Good. Are we staying long?

For tea, Willy's mother said. We've been asked for tea.

Willy's father opened the door and they went out to the car. Willy's mother got into the front seat and lit a cigarette. Willy got into the back seat and wound down the window. For months now he had been haunted by fear whenever he sat in a car. He was prone to fear. He was afraid of foxes, of earthquakes, of the dreadful giraffe his mother said came down the back stairs. His fear of cars dated from a dream he had at school. He dreamed that he was sitting in the back seat of their old green car, the one with the windscreen that wound open, his mother and father in the front. They were moving easily forward, with none of the usual concomitants of driving, no engine noise, no gear changes, no shift of weight as they went round corners. They came to a long, straight, steep hill, and were gliding up it when, for no apparent reason, and with no reaction from his parents, the car stopped, and rolled sickeningly backwards. Whenever he dreamed this dream Willy woke frozen with terror, and he never got into a car without fear. When they came to a hill it was all he could do not to cry out. In order to conceal this fear he pretended to be car-sick, and often spent whole journeys with his head out of the window, gulping air.

Willy's father stood at the car door, and when Willy wound down the window he reached in and tousled his hair.

All right, Noddle? he said.

Willy gave what he hoped was a brave smile, and his father got into the car and started up. Willy leaned out of the window.

As they drove through the village Willy reflected on his fear. Really, he felt, it was just another way in which life changed after you went to school. In the days which preceded the nightmare Willy had enjoyed driving. He had enjoyed the way his parents laughed and joked in the front. His mother would sit sideways with her arm along the back of the seat. Sometimes she would stroke his father's shoulder. Sometimes she would glance back at Willy and they would share a smile. If Willy leaned out of the window then it was to wave at passers-by, and sing. Today his mother faced the front.

Willy had discovered that he loved his father in this very car. They had gone to Salisbury on business, and stopped on the way back to buy apples. The journey had passed, as journeys with his father always did, in silence. Willy was mildly bored. As they drove away from the fruit shop they were overtaken noisily by a sports car, and Willy's father swore. Munching apples they drove on till they were stopped, after about a mile, by roadworks, and pulled up behind the sports car.

He didn't get very far, Willy's father said. For all his farting fury.

Willy laughed.

No he didn't get very far, his father said. He liked to repeat things if he found them funny, savouring them. For all his farting fury.

Willy laughed and laughed and choked on his apple. His father slapped him on the back and they laughed and Willy realized: this is Daddy. This is my father. I am laughing with my father whom I love. Then a workman came and waved them on, and they drove home.

In the light of this recollection, Willy inspected his father's profile through the window. He found that he could recall none of the former emotion. A tense-jawed stranger gripped the steering wheel. He looked away and caught his father's eye in the wing mirror. His father's eye winked at him, and he withdrew into the car.

Well, Willy's mother said. I wonder what it's going to be today.

The best thing, his father said, would be to wait and see. Don't you think?

Willy's mother stubbed out her cigarette.

These make me feel sick, she said.

You shouldn't anyway, his father said. Not in your condition.

If it's money again I shall scream, his mother said. After last time.

He is my brother, Willy's father said. Everything is half his. Legally.

Legally, Willy's mother said.

The car approached the foot of a steep hill, and Willy stopped listening, and held his breath. Half-way up the hill the car stalled, and stopped. They rolled backwards down the hill for a few feet till Willy's father put on the brake. Willy gasped and jumped in his seat.

Willy, whatever is the matter? his mother said.

It's all right, his father said. She's just a bit cold. That's all. We'll soon get her going again.

Willy, who had just noticed that he wasn't at all afraid, laughed and said: Nothing. It just made me jump. Nothing.

Willy's father started the car again, and Willy leant out of the window and sang. The car mounted the hill and sped down the other side, and Willy sang and sang:

My body lies over the ocean.
My body lies over the sea.

94

Bring back, Oh bring back,
Oh bring back my body to me.

He sang into the slipstream, and played his favourite car-game of imagining that the wheels were scythed, and lopped down trees and telegraph poles as they passed. He turned and sang right into the rushing wind, and laughed when its force stopped his breath and made him turn back.

Speed bonny boat, he sang, Like a bird on the wing, Over the sea to Skye.

Willy, his mother said. Willy! Stop it. You're making my head reel.

It had not occurred to Willy that his singing could be heard within the car. He had thought the slipstream carried his words away. He drew back into the car, furiously blushing.

And close the window, his mother said. I'm getting a stiff neck.

She twitched at her coat collar, and Willy wound up the window. His mother lit another cigarette. Willy sat with his hands clenched in his lap and waited for his blush to fade. The car wheels, he noticed, were still scything down telegraph poles. He could imagine them bouncing on the suspending wires as they fell. This distracted him and he unclenched his hands.

I bet it's money, Willy's mother said. It's always money. Anyone would think we were made of money.

I still think we ought to wait and see, Willy's father said.

It isn't right, Willy's mother said. You carry almost all of the business. I warn you. If you give in like last time I shall be furious.

She wound down her window and threw out her cigarette.

God, she said. They taste awful. I feel sick.

She leaned out and breathed deeply. Then she drew her head back in and massaged her neck.

I hate this, she said. I really hate this.

She wound up the window, then wound it down again.

I'm going to be sick, she said.

Willy's father stopped the car, and Willy's mother got out and bent over the verge. Willy shifted to his mother's side of the car and watched her out of the window. Willy's father got out and went over to his wife. He put his arm round her shoulder. She pulled away from him and vomited. Willy watched her shoulders heave and began to feel sick himself. He leaned back and closed his eyes. His father led his mother back to the car. She got in and sat with her head bent between her knees. Willy's father squatted on his heels and spoke through the window.

Shall we go home? he said.

Willy's mother sat up.

No, she said. We've got this far.

Sure? his father said.

Sure, his mother said.

Willy sat forward and opened his eyes.

All right, Noddle? his father said.

All right, Willy said.

Right, his father said, and stood up.

Right, he said again, and walked round the car, and got into his seat, and slammed the door.

Right, he said, and started up and drove off.

It isn't my fault, Willy's mother said.

Christ, Willy's father said. And again, more quietly, Christ.

It was the last thing anyone said till they turned, quarter of an hour later, into Willy's uncle's yard, and Willy saw Diddle waiting for them.

Hello Diddle, Willy's father said.

Hello Uncle, Diddle said. Can Willy play for a while before tea?

I don't see why not, Willy's father said. Off you go, Willy.

Willy and Diddle stood side by side, and watched Willy's father and mother walk past the Dutch barn towards the house.

Mummy was sick, Willy said. By the side of the road.

Never mind, Diddle said. Let's go to the camp. You could have a cigarette.

You're not supposed to smoke if you're going to have a baby, Willy said.

That's just women, Diddle said. Don't you know anything?

Come and have a look at the camp. I've made some improvements.

What time is tea? Willy said.

Plenty of time, Diddle said.

And he led Willy into the Dutch barn.

The Dutch barn was a huge construction of girders and corrugated metal. It housed, at one end, Willy's uncle's farm machinery. Diddle led Willy past tractors and balers, ploughs and combine harvesters. The other end was entirely occupied by bales of straw, packed to the roof. To reach Diddle's camp you had to climb, as they now did, up the bales to an opening at the top right-hand edge, where an accident of storage had left a gap between the straw and the roof that formed a tunnel the depth of the barn. At the end of the tunnel, into which Willy watched Diddle disappear, the space opened out into a room-sized area, lit by a plastic window in the roof. Here Diddle had arranged bales into seats and tables. Here he kept his airgun, his cigarettes, and his transistor radio. And here, Willy remembered as he paused on the baleface at the tunnel's entry, peering into the dark for a sight of Diddle's heels, Diddle conducted his experiments. Here, on his last visit, Diddle had sucked Willy's willy, and made Willy suck his, which had left a not unpleasant india-rubber sensation that lingered in the mouth for some hours. Here too, Willy recalled as he hoisted himself into the tunnel and wriggled forward on his elbows, Diddle had performed the operation known as sticking the willy in the jelly, which involved Willy's lying face down and naked on a bale while Diddle lay naked on top of him. This last, although accompanied by no noticeable sensation other than weight and the prickle of straw against the belly, Willy was determined not to allow him to repeat. Diddle's subsequent announcement that now he, Willy, would have a baby, seemed to amuse Diddle no end but had filled Willy, still filled him, with consternation.

There was a moment, half-way along the tunnel, when the light from one end gave out, and the light from the other was not yet visible. Here Willy stopped, and breathed deeply to fight off

panic. He lay flat on his face on the straw. The same feeling overtook him as had overtaken him sometimes when he woke in the
middle of the night in the days before the nightlight: a feeling of
pushing a bulbous weight, coupled with a sort of gigantism of the
limbs. His arms, his legs, his chest, all felt sluggish and turgid, as
if thickly encased in bone. His joints ground and groaned. He
connected this feeling with Diddle's assertion that he was going
to have a baby and, somehow, with his mother's inflated
stomach. He thought he might be sick. He resisted the urge and
wriggled forward. Soon he emerged into light, and there was
Diddle smiling at him.

Well, Diddle said. What do you think?

Willy blinked.

How did you do it? he said.

I did it by myself, Diddle said. Nobody else knows. It took a
long time.

The camp was transformed. What had been simply a random
space was squared off, and organized. There were deck-chairs at
one end, next to two bales pushed together, with an old Persian
carpet thrown over them, for a table. Three more bales at the opposite end, with a sleeping bag on top of them, formed a bed.
There was a bentwood coat rack, and posters on the wall. In a
niche in the breeze-blocked barn wall above the bed was a stuffed
owl in a glass case.

It's not finished of course, Diddle said. But I think it's going to
be good, don't you?

It's great, Willy said.

I spend a lot of time here, Diddle said. I got fed up with scruffi-
ness. You can't be messy all your life. Sit down.

Willy sat on one of the deck-chairs.

Make yourself at home, Diddle said. Would you like a drink
before tea? I've got Coke, or Tizer, or lemonade. It'll have to be
paper cups, I'm afraid.

Tizer please, Willy said.

I was only joking about the cigarettes, Diddle said. I've given
up. But you can if you like. I've got an ashtray somewhere.

No thanks, Willy said.

Good man, Diddle said.

He poured Willy's Tizer, and a Coke for himself, and sat in the other deck-chair.

Thanks, Willy said.

Like I said, Diddle said, I got fed up with messiness. You've got to grow up sometime.

Yes, Willy said. Yes, you have.

Well then, Diddle said. What have you been up to?

Nothing much, Willy said. I go back to school in eleven days. I don't like my school.

Mine's all right, Diddle said. You should try it.

I wish I could, Willy said. They ring bells all the time. Bells to get up in the morning. Bells at night. Bells for lessons. Bells for meals. It gives you a headache. You're not allowed to talk in the corridors. I hate it.

You'll get used to it, Diddle said.

They play football, Willy said.

I like football, Diddle said. It's good for you.

Yes, Willy said. Like cabbage. Cabbage is good for you too.

Willy's father's voice suddenly sounded, surprisingly near, through the wall of the barn.

Willy! his father's voice said. Willy!

It must be tea-time, Diddle said. Drink up.

Willy! his father's voice said. Willy, come here! Where are you?

Coming Uncle, Diddle called.

Hurry up, Willy's father said.

You first, Diddle said. I'll stay and tidy up a bit and be along in a minute.

Willy climbed back into the tunnel and crawled along it. The return passage was easier though he still felt a bit panicky in the dark centre. He climbed down the bales, and made his way past the machinery to the barn entrance. His father stood at the door, facing outwards.

Willy! he shouted. Come on!

Here I am, Willy said.

99

Willy's father span round. His face was very red.

Come on, he said. We're going.

Is it tea-time? Willy said.

Forget tea, his father said. We're going.

Willy's mother was sitting in the car.

No, Willy said. No. We've only just come.

Willy, will you come on, his father said.

It's not fair, Willy said. We've only just come.

For God's sake, Willy, his father said. Will you do what you're told.

No, Willy said. I won't. It's not fair.

He turned away from his father and ran round the barn. Behind the barn was a small copse, and behind that a field. Willy's father caught up with Willy in the middle of the field. He grabbed Willy by the back of his pullover, turned him round, and hit him several times with the flat of his hand over the head and shoulders.

There! he said. There! Now do what you're bloody well told.

At the third stroke Willy burst into tears. Then he fell to his knees and cowered. Willy's father bent down and hit him again. He pulled him to his feet and dragged him back across the field. As they entered the copse Willy shook his shoulder from his father's grasp. His father stopped, crouched down so that his head was level with Willy's, and held him by the waist. Willy felt his hands shaking.

Now look Willy, he said. Pretty soon you're going to be in big trouble. Right? Just stop it. Right?

He walked back to the car. Sniffing, Willy dried his eyes. Then he followed his father to the car. He sat bolt upright in the middle of the back seat. Diddle stood by the barn entrance, watching, but Willy kept looking straight ahead.

Willy wondered, as his father slammed the back door on him, why he had cried. It hadn't hurt. At least not much. Not enough to cry for. It had been unfair. But not enough to cry for. Strangely enough, he thought, his muscles tensed against the force of his father's acceleration, it had been fear. How odd to be afraid in the middle of something rather than before. But afraid is what he had been. Afraid of the blaze of rage that whirled above him. It hadn't hurt. Actually now it was quite nice. His head and shoulders glowed pleasantly warm.

Willy sank down in his seat. He put his hands in his pockets. In his right pocket he found the tissue and his mother's tube of lipstick. His fingers closed round the tube. He leant back his head and listened to the beating of his heart and the pulse of blood in his ears.

THE GENERAL'S TOOTHACHE

The General, although a skilful marksman, had never seen active service. His was a political promotion, the reward for administrative excellence. His knighthood, bestowed on the last Birthday, had caused ill feeling, young as he was.

The General, then, left the War Office at half past five. At Victoria station he bought a two-pound box of Terry's All Gold chocolates, some coloured wrapping paper, and a roll of matching ribbon. In the forward first-class carriage of the six thirty-five to Pulborough he wrapped the chocolates, bound the parcel with ribbon, and, in his own special way, a way he was particularly proud of, involving as it did no Sellotape or adhesive of any kind, contrived a meticulous and elaborate bow. His wife met him at Pulborough station, and drove him home. Over sherry before dinner he presented her with the parcel, which she unwrapped carefully, folding the wrapping paper, and winding the ribbon into a neat hank. After dinner, at the General's prompting, she opened the box, and they had two chocolates each, with their brandy, before going to bed.

Later, at about two o'clock, the General, who had trouble sleeping, came down to the drawing room for a second brandy, and helped himself to a third chocolate. He sipped his brandy, and sucked his chocolate. It was not one of his favourites. As a rule he preferred soft-centred fruity ones. On this occasion he had been careless, and selected at random what turned out to be a mixture of caramel and nuts. Shortly he tired of sucking and decided to chew. He bit down hard, and dislodged a filling in a lower left molar. He swore, swallowed the chocolate without further chewing, washed it down with the remains of his brandy, and went to bed.

Next morning the General woke with a toothache, which worsened during the course of the day. In the afternoon he telephoned his dentist, and was told that the first available appointment was in ten days' time. He made the appointment and bought a packet of Anadin. By evening, however, the pain in his tooth was so intense that the recommended dose of two pills every two hours was inadequate to cope with it, and he stepped the number up to three. He woke several times during the night. The next day the General exceeded the maximum dose by a hundred per cent, and still the tooth ached.

On the morning of the third day the General decided that he could take no more, and telephoned his dentist for an emergency appointment. Unfortunately, the receptionist said, his dentist was away and would not be back till the morning of the Tuesday when the General was to see him anyway. However, if it really was an emergency an appointment could be arranged with one of the junior partners for five o'clock that evening. The General assured the receptionist that it was a genuine emergency. He would be there at five o'clock. He took three more Anadin, rested his head in his hands, and fell asleep at his desk.

The dentist's partner looked at the General's tooth, and asked him what sort of pain he felt. The General was unable to specify, beyond the fact that the pain was continuous and acute. The dentist rapped his lower left molars in turn. The General howled. Yes, the dentist said, he had damaged a nerve. Not to worry. It was a relatively easy matter to relieve the pressure. Just a bit of drilling here, and in the tooth above, to minimize contact. The tooth, of course, was much filled, almost all metal in fact, and he would probably have to lose it. But all that could wait till the General's dentist got back. Snap your teeth together now.

The General snapped his teeth together and the pain abated. It was not until he was again sitting in the forward first-class carriage to Pulborough that it returned with redoubled vigour, and increased as the journey continued to the point of agony. The General's wife met him at the station as usual, and drove him straight to the casualty unit of the local hospital, where he was given enough of a stronger painkiller to get him through the night, and firm instructions to go back to his dentist the next day. It took an hour for the pills to work, during which time the pain spread to the whole of the left side of his face, his jaw, his cheek, his ear, his eye, even his nose.

Unwilling to return to the dentist he regarded as responsible for this increase in pain, the General presented himself the next morning at the emergency clinic at the Royal Dental Hospital in Leicester Square. There they X-rayed his jaw, pronounced the offending tooth rotten, and extracted it. The General, who was mightily afraid of needles, welcomed nevertheless the blissful numbness of lignocaine, and concentrated on the beauty of the view over the square, as a student worked at his tooth. He looked forward, he told the student, to being able to get back to work. He had shamefully neglected it. He had a very important meeting with the Minister that afternoon.

It was during this meeting that the lignocaine wore off, and the pain returned, worse even than before. The General had to be helped, writhing, from the room. He immediately took six Anadin, and after an hour, when the pain had still not decreased, six more. Every particle of the left side of his face, from his fore-head to the base of his throat, was aflame. Eventually the Anadin had some effect, and he had a staff car drive him home. When he arrived he went straight to bed, and slept and ate painkillers by turns. He did not notice his wife's arrival. When he woke in the morning he was cradled in her arms.

The General devoted the following days to striving unsuccess-fully to establish a *modus vivendi* with his pain. At the best of times he was not a man to whom the law of cause and effect was obvious. He rarely connected, for example, the fact that he was not hungry with the meal he had just eaten. He was simply either hungry or not hungry. That was all. So it was with his toothache. He found it difficult to connect the fact that his tooth ached less with the handful of pills he had just taken to lessen its aching. He never expected the pain to return, and it always did. And he had always forgotten just how painful it was. It always took an hour for the next batch of pills to work. Two days passed before he came to terms with this, and admitted that he was going to have to take the pills at regular intervals. He took six Anadin every four

hours, and eight before he slept at night. This made him coma-
tose. His head throbbed, his eyes bulged, his bowels heaved. But
it was better than the pain.

The General had never before had to do with severe pain;
indeed, apart from the occasional headache, the odd twinge of
piles, and a fractured metacarpal while still at school, he was a
stranger to even its milder forms. How little a description of his
present state the word toothache was, with its vague associations
with a visiting niece's childish pangs easily soothable with a dab
of whisky on the afflicted area and a hug from her aunt. This pain
bewildered him by its sheer tenacity. Nothing would drive it
away. Even under the strongest painkillers he had yet taken it
was still there, an echo, a leaden *ostinato* to all he did. And every
now and again some part of his face would be transfixed with a
stabbing agony. He kept his left eye permanently closed.

Nor was the pain his only problem. He found the absence of his
tooth almost impossible to bear. His tongue sought out and
probed the pulpy socket, and he had no control over the movement of his cheek, which was continually pulled into the gap, and
often bitten by the surrounding teeth. The teeth themselves
seemed to be re-aligning in his mouth. They tingled, and would
not fit together with their accustomed comfort. They dragged in
conflicting directions, and tugged with them the musculature of
his jaw and throat. His tongue no longer fitted in his mouth, and
the space between his teeth felt lumpish and obtrusive, as if he
were constantly sucking a boiled sweet, and made him retch. He
could eat little. He found too that the whole variety of oral stimu-
lants, from which he usually derived comfort and pleasure, was
impossible for him to enjoy, though he still craved them. Smoking
filled him with nausea. Alcohol actually made him vomit. The
thought of solid food made his stomach churn. He subsisted on
tepid soup, weak milkless tea, and Turkish Delight, which he
palped with his tongue against his palate. Kissing his wife, even
the modest peck on the cheek that her love and sympathy over
this period required, underlined for him his position as an
unwhole, unwholesome man, and overwhelmed him with self-

loathing. He developed a stye in his left eye, and felt sure his breath stank. The last two days before his appointment with his own dentist on Tuesday he spent in bed, nursing his jaw, waiting, and enduring.

On the Monday night the General fell asleep in his wife's arms – it had become her custom to cradle him since the dreadful night of his return from the Dental Hospital, although she was careful not to kiss him – and dreamed: He was a dog, curled up at night, under the stars, by some Asiatic campfire. Men in turbans also sat round the fire, cracking nuts and telling stories. Strangers approached, and the leader of the General's band stood up to welcome them, leaning on his spear. He did not notice that its butt was thrusting into his dog's thigh. The General endured the weight of the butt for as long as he could, then lashed out at it with his teeth. His wife was wakened by his snarl in time to receive a vicious snap across the muzzle from the General's teeth, which fastened on to her nose. She pulled back her face, dragged the General's teeth from her nose, and struck him with the full force of her arm on the mouth. The General, still asleep, wailed and buried his face between her breasts. She soothed him, stroking his hair, until he woke, her body shaking with laughter. She told him what had happened, and they both, groggy with sleep and the strangeness of the occurrence, shrieked with laughter for several minutes. Then the General's wife went to wash the blood from her nose, where his teeth had broken the skin. As she walked to the bathroom the General noticed the tired droop of her shoulders, the sag of her ageing breasts, and was filled with such tenderness that, on her return, they made love for the first time since his toothache had started. Afterwards the General slept peacefully for the first time in as long a period.

His wife drove him up to town the following morning to see his dentist. The dentist inspected his mouth, syringed his empty socket, and filled it with antiseptic wadding. The pain immediately ceased. The General lay in the dentist's chair, engulfed in relief. For fully a minute he could not move. Then he thanked the dentist, and his wife drove him home. He passed the day euphoric with happiness, and in the evening took his wife, her nose carefully made up to conceal his toothmarks, out to dinner. On the way home from dinner his tooth started aching again. When they arrived he sent his wife up to bed, saying that he would join her shortly, and sat in the drawing room, clutching his jaw. After an hour he went up to his bedroom. His wife had fallen asleep over a book. He closed the book and put it on her bedside table. Carefully he kissed her carefully made-up nose, and went downstairs to his study. There he took his pistol from his desk, loaded it, and directed into his mouth the first shot he had ever fired in anger.

WH'APPEN?

One

On the day of the Paris–Brest au Café he became a man. After breakfast, while he was taking the ingredients out of the fridge and packing them in his satchel, his mother sat dry-eyed and straight-backed at the table and told him. His father, she said, would not be joining them. He was staying in Nairobi. It was he, her son, who was the man of the family now.

He liked cooking. He felt clean when he was cooking. He could forget things while he was cooking. But you can't cook all the time. You can make bigger, and better, and longer, and more complicated dishes, but the time still comes when you have to close the oven, even if only for fifteen minutes with the door propped open with a spoon, as in the Paris–Brest au Café, but you had to close it, and wait. He filled the time as best he could, preparing the next stage of the dish if there were one, washing up if there weren't. He did all the washing up he could. He did the whole class's washing up whenever it was possible, which wasn't often, because Miss McLeod wouldn't let him. She wouldn't let him be used as a servant, she said. He shouldn't let himself be used as a servant. He should stand up for himself. He had talent. A real flair. He should be proud.

He had tried to explain. Before he became a man he had tried to explain. Then he didn't try any more, because men don't have to explain anything. He liked the washing up, he had said. He enjoyed it, really he did. But Miss McLeod had seen the way the others treated him. She had seen the covert, and not so covert, kicks, the cuffs, the pushes, the whispered giggling taunts. And she wasn't going to have anyone bullied into an unfair share of the work in her class, certainly not her ablest pupil, the only one with any real gift. So he couldn't do the washing up. And the time came when he had put away the last bowl, hung up the last tea

towel, and he had to wait. And while he was waiting he couldn't
forget things any more. He couldn't forget his father in Kenya,
whom he wasn't going to see again. He couldn't forget his dry-
eyed, straight-backed mother, cardiganed and slippered against
the cold. He couldn't forget that you could travel for miles and
hours in London without seeing anything that wasn't London,
that the air was dank and dirty and unpleasant to breathe. He
couldn't forget that, at school, wherever he was there was never
anyone else, that there was always a gap between himself and the
children, and the children hissed and spat on the other side of it.
Paki, they called him, and Bent cunt, and Wanker. It made nothing easier, being a man. And they only had Cooking once a week
anyway.

His name was Télémaque Dieudonné Pombal. Pombal because
his father's family, before they had emigrated to become tailors in
Mombasa and later wholesale clothes dealers in Nairobi, had
been Portuguese, from Goa. Télémaque because his father said
they had waited for him for a long time, and French was the
language of Reason. Dieudonné because his mother had prayed
and prayed, for years and years, she and the French Sisters of the
Sacred Heart in Nairobi, that he should be conceived, and lit thou-
sands of candles, she and the French Sisters of the Holy Wounds
in Mombasa, where her family lived, where she had been sent
during her pregnancy, that he should be carried to term, and he
had been, and French was the language of God. He had few memories of Kenya. His mother had a book of photographs, but even
in the days before his manhood he had looked at them only
rarely. They meant little. He could not connect them with himself.
He knew, he could see, that that house was his house, that that
man was his father, but it meant nothing to him. He felt nothing.
Similarly his memory, before his manhood forbade him to ask it,
would play over for him images which, though he recognized
them, found no answering chime in his feelings. Which, in some
cases, his reason told him were inaccurate. As when he remembered that the staircase that led from his to his parents' bedroom
had descended from left to right, when the photographs told him

– there he was, sitting on the stairs, smiling at his father behind the camera – that it descended from right to left. As when the photographs showed him a smiling man who loved his family, and yet his father had sent him to England without saying why, had promised to join him and had not joined him, had dried his mother's eyes and stiffened her back with pain – his father whom he would never see again or know if he saw him. But when he became a man he put away childish things. He never looked at his mother's photographs. He turned his back on his memory. Soon all that remained of his past was a bodily memory of heat, a craving in his bones for dry in this chilly, shabby land, or, if he must be cold, for the crystal cold of a Kenyan morning, when the nostrils stung.

And his dreams.

He had two dreams. It felt as if he dreamed them every night, sometimes one, sometimes one after the other, sometimes a sickening jumble of the two. When he woke it was with a constriction in his throat that he would have characterized – had anyone asked him, and his mother carefully did not, and who else was there? – as wanting to yawn and not being able to, until life at school taught him to recognize it for what it was: fear and unshed tears. The first dream was the shorter. In it he and his mother and Soeur Geneviève from the Holy Wounds were decorating the Christmas crib in the convent chapel in Mombasa. They laid the figure of the Christ child in his manger on shredded paper painted to look like straw, and Saint Joseph and the Virgin beside him. Soeur Geneviève unrolled the dark blue canvas sky, and lighted the blue bulb that shed a cold northern light, and the yellow one that gave the inside of the crib its cosy glow. They laid the Ox and the Ass in their positions behind the manger, and the fleece-clad Shepherds with strange northern sheep on their shoulders. His mother mantled the roof with sifted sugar which gave, she said, the authentic sparkle of snow. He hated this dream. The second was not much better. It began with walking. It was a still clear morning in the hills near Karamoja where they went every year around the time of his father's birthday. He and his father walked. They walked, and walked, and walked, and fell into that long loping bound that comes when you feel the earth swing to the rhythm of your feet. They climbed higher and higher into the hills. It got colder and clearer as they rose, until they breasted the final summit and looked down into a shallow valley filled to the brim like a bowl with mist. We have to go down, his father said, to go higher, and pointed out over the valley to where a grove of treetops thrust up out of the mist. And they went down. At least he thought it was they, but before long he realized it was just he. The mist was clammy, stifling and cold, like a wet flannel across the mouth. It tangled his legs and would not let him walk. It muffled his ears. He tried to shout but it swallowed his voice. He struggled forward pace after pace and in the end he found himself groping at the base of a great tree. The trunk of the tree was smooth and its lowest branch beyond his reach, but he knew he had to climb it, and circled its base trying to work out how.

He was thirteen years old.

Two

It didn't take him long to see how it was. On his first day he saw how it was. He was a Late Arrival. They came from Kenya at the end of September, and it was November before he went to school. He sat in the middle of the room and watched what happened around him. These were the days before his manhood, so he observed closely and tried to learn the rules. The rules weren't so difficult. By lunch-time, after five lessons and a break, Salimi had shown him how it was.

Div! Farley said.

Who's a div? Salimi said.

You're a div, div! Farley said.

I'm not a div, Salimi said.

The words didn't seem to mean much, apart from their tone. The tone conveyed what they meant. So did the punch to the shoulder that accompanied them.

Div! Farley said. Tramp! Pouf! Flid! Plonker! Paki! Cunt! Dildo!

I'm not, Salimi said.

What aren't you, dildo? Farley said. Which one aren't you, cunt?

What you said, Salimi said.

What did I say, wanker? Farley said.

Paki, Salimi said.

So who's a Paki? Farley said.

I'm not a Paki, Salimi said.

Well one of us here is, Farley said, and it's not me.

I'm not a Paki, Salimi said.

So it's me then, is it? Farley said. I'm a Paki then, am I? You're calling me a Paki, then are you?

The punch to the shoulder became a cuff round the back of the head.

Suck my dick, plonker! Farley said. Nobody calls me a Paki. Sit on my prick, pouf!

I didn't, Salimi said.

So I'm a liar too, am I? Farley said. Your mother sucks, cunt! Eat your mother's Tampax, bender! Eat your mother's pussy, Paki!

Salimi picked up his chair.

You leave my mother out of it, he said.

Make me, Farley said. You make me.

He knocked the chair out of Salimi's hands.

Come on then, he said. Come on. Or can't Pakis fight then? Or are they all women like their mothers? Their fucking Paki bitch mothers.

Salimi flew at him. Instantly their grappling bodies were surrounded by a swaying stamping crowd, clapping and chanting:

Fight!

Fight!

Fight!

In the playground, during break, it happened again. From the corner of a building, where he stood hunched under the hood of his anorak against the wet and the strangeness, he saw Salimi crouched on the ground, while Farley and some others he didn't know yet circled round him shouting:

Salimi, Salami! Salimi, Salami!

He saw it was only a matter of time before it happened to him. He wondered how he would feel. He wondered how he would react.

He didn't realize his mistake until it was too late. He felt pain, of course, and rage, and rejection, and bitter loneliness. But it didn't matter what he felt. It didn't matter how he reacted. The trick was to react. Nothing, he knew after a time, would have stopped them. He could have wept and begged. It wouldn't have mattered. He could have threatened, cringed, cajoled, fought back. It would have made no difference to them. They would simply have gone on and on until they got bored or found someone else, as had happened with Salimi, whom he saw every now and again looking at him under his eyebrows from across the room. They had no choice. They spoke the only language they knew. But for his own sake it would have been better to react. Impassivity, though forced on him initially by shock and then kept up in an attempt at dignity, was a mistake. Impassivity goaded his attackers to an even greater fury, and concentrated the fury on him in an effort to break it. Impassivity, when his tie was being tightened slowly round his throat to make him hand over his dinner money, was a hard act to maintain. But most of all impassivity was a lie. To pretend that he wasn't feeling what he could not fail to feel distanced him less from the pain than from reality. To deny what he felt was to deny, he felt, his existence. He wanted to change. He intended to change. But then his manhood descended and trapped him.

He endured. In the playground he was hunted or alone. In the classroom his pens were stolen, his pencil box torn in two, his books scribbled on, his bag thrown round the room, his work stolen. He was punched, kicked, cursed. He spent much time crying in the lavatory. He told no one. But it was noticed. Miss McLeod noticed. On the day of the Paris–Brest au Café she spoke to Mr Gilbert, his housemaster, and together, that evening, they spoke to Mrs Inchbald, his tutor, and for the next few weeks they all watched very carefully, and Mrs Inchbald tried to talk to him.

She kept him back after the others had gone and asked him how he was getting on. She gave him odd jobs to do around the tutor room and talked about this and that. Once, on her way home, she stopped her car and offered him a lift. He refused. He was not deceived. He knew what she wanted, but men do not yield up their secrets to prying eyes. Men do not complain or explain. Men treat each other with respect. They pay each other the compliment of assuming that they are in control, that they can cope, that they know what they are doing, that they can carry the weight of their lives. It was not his fault if his teacher was a stranger to this elementary point of honour. Mrs Inchbald wrote a letter to his mother. His mother read it at the breakfast table and showed it to him. He read it, tossed back his head and glared. His mother prepared a special meal for him after school, but he would not eat it. He poked at it, found fault with a sauce, and pushed it away. He did not need kindness. He was a man.

The next day, by way of a test, he was rude to the referee during the Wednesday morning football game, and was ordered from the field. After the match the referee spoke to him kindly. Mrs Inchbald had obviously been talking. He wondered how, on top of everything else, he could bear the shame.

Three

Junior Senior told him about the Grand Master. You think you have problems, he said. You should try mine. You should try holding out against them, man. You should hear the things they call you then, man. See the things they do to you then. You could tell the Grand Master by their uniform: a white T-shirt with a black sign in summer, a black sweat-shirt with a white sign in winter, and tall white trainers with high tongues, the trousers tucked behind the tongue. The sign said Wh'appen? in big letters across the chest. Wh'appen? was the sign. You were black and they asked you, and they didn't ask just anyone, you wore the sign or you were in big trouble. Junior Senior didn't wear the sign. They hadn't asked him yet, but he knew they were going to.

He'd seen the right people talking to the right people about him. The right people had brushed up against him in the playground. He wasn't dumb. The main reason they wanted him was he wasn't dumb. He could save them a lot of time. He didn't want to wear the sign. He just didn't know if he could hold out.

He first saw Junior Senior looking at him in Cookery class the first week back after Christmas. He was washing up. I see you, Junior Senior's eyes said. I see what you're doing. You and I should get together. Two heads are better than one. Soon, whenever he looked up, there was Junior Senior looking at him. He didn't like it. It got on his nerves. In the end it got so he couldn't stand it, and he went up to Junior Senior in the playground and said: What you keep looking at me for? You bent or what?

That's right, Junior Senior said. Let it out. Let it all out.

Let what out, div? he said. Let what out, plonker? You gay or what?

He jabbed Junior Senior in the ribs with stiffened fingers. Junior Senior rolled with the jab.

OK, Junior Senior said. All right.

Shitface, he said. Tramp! Wanker! Dildo! Cunt! I shit on your mother's face. I spit on your mother's grave.

You left one out, Junior Senior said. You didn't say Paki.

Bright, he said. Clever. How can I call you a Paki when you're not a Paki? So shame!

No shame, Junior Senior said. You're not a Paki either. And I wouldn't be ashamed if I was.

He drew back his hand for a punch. Junior Senior did not move.

You mustn't disappoint them, Junior Senior said. The first time you've got them on your side you mustn't let them down.

He noticed the crowd for the first time.

They're hoping for a fight, Junior Senior said. It would be a pity to let them down.

The crowd swelled. From all over the playground the children came running. They jostled and barged in a ring round him and Junior Senior, jockeying for the best view.

They're here for a fight, Junior Senior said. Shall we give them a fight? I'd say we have about half a minute before a teacher arrives. Fifteen seconds for him to push through the crowd. Ten seconds to drag us apart. Shall we put on a show?

Junior Senior put up his fists and danced in front of him, shouting: Come on! Come on! Put them up and fight!

Fight, the crowd shouted.

Put them up, Junior Senior shouted. Put them up and fight.

Fight! they shouted again. Fight! Fight!

You can't get away, Junior Senior said. You're surrounded. What are you going to do?

Fight!

He stood. He let his arms drop to his side. Junior Senior moved a step forward.

All right, Junior Senior said. OK.

He hung his head. His shoulders shook.

Mr Blunt pushed his way through the crowd.

All right, all right, he said. Come on. Break it up. What's going on here?

Nothing, Junior Senior said. My friend tripped and fell, that's all. He'll be all right in a minute.

Well? Mr Blunt said. Well?

He'll be all right soon, Junior Senior said.

Shut up you, Mr Blunt said. I'm talking to him. Well? What have you got to say?

It's all right, he said. I'm all right.

Quite a crowd-gathering thing, tripping and falling, Mr Blunt said. What a touching display of concern. How glad you must be to have so many people rush to take care of you.

Yes, he said. Yes.

Nice to be so popular, Mr Blunt said. I wish I was so popular.

Can I take him in, sir, Junior Senior said.

Oh well, Mr Blunt said. Why not? Come on, the rest of you. Show's over.

Junior Senior put his arm round his shoulder and took him in.

You mustn't think, Junior Senior said, that just because they've got a silly name they're not every bit as tough as they think they are. If they ask me to wear the sign it's just a question of time before I wear it. In many ways they have the right idea. Unity is strength. All that. I mean, you beat up on a member and see what happens to you. You're the biggest, strongest, toughest, whitest boy in the school and you beat up on a member, and you meet twenty or thirty Grand Master on the way home, you're not going to get through unchanged. No, man! But they use it wrong. Where they find hate and fear they throw it right back. They trade in hate and fear, all in the name of black solidarity at best, or self-defence if they're feeling a bit more honest, but all they are is gangsters, and trade is mostly what they're interested in. Even their own kind, the ordinary everyday black guys. They don't wear the sign, they're fair game. They get harassed. Their money gets stolen. They get hustled for protection, the same as the white guys. It's just another power structure to deal with. They want me. They want me because I'm bright. Because they've heard I'm bright. But are they going to use me, use that brightness? Hell, no. They want me to do the King's work for him. They want me to do the King's maths homework, with just the right convincing amount of right convincing mistakes, so the teacher will lay off the King for a bit, and free him to extort enough money for the Space Invaders, or a new pair of Nikes, or an Armani jacket, or whatever he thinks is going to make him cooler and hipper than all the rest, cool enough and hip enough to stay the King. I shall try. I shall try to stay out when they ask me. But I don't hold out any hope. A few days' grace at most.

They sat in the Cookery room. Miss McLeod had spoken with Mrs Inchbald, and together they had taken their idea to Mr Gilbert: Give the boy a sanctuary; give him a space just to be; by himself, preferably, or maybe with the friend he seems to have made himself; somewhere to work at what he's good at. Miss McLeod could keep a discreet eye on things. So after school they met in the Cookery room, and he showed Junior Senior how to cook, and Junior Senior helped him with his homework. Miss McLeod popped in and out on one pretext or another, and shooed away the children who every now and again gathered at the door to call

Bender! and Pouf! and How's your new boyfriend? before they got bored and went home. Junior Senior told him about Jamaica, where he had not been but greatly hoped to go, and he told Junior Senior about Kenya and the airless English cold. Junior Senior explained that his father was called Junior Senior too, so that he was really Junior Senior Junior, and he told Junior Senior about Dieudonné and Télémaque. Junior Senior told him about the Grand Master and Wh'appen? and he told Junior Senior, gradually and with difficulty, about his dreams, about his mother, about his father, and finally about his manhood. If he was lucky there was no one waiting for him on the way home.

After February half term he went to see the King. He told Junior Senior nothing about it. One break he ran the gauntlet of the Wh'appen? shirts and went to the lavatories down by the swimming pool where the King held his winter court.

What the fuck you want, poison-shit? the Wh'appen? shirts said. You got nerve, man. You got face coming here, Paki-rat. Get the fuck away back home.

I've come to see the King, he said. I've got something for him. I've got an idea.

So the Paki-rat's got an idea, man, they said. Who the fuck wants a Paki idea? Go eat curried shit, man.

The King took off his dark glasses, looked at him, and put them back on again. The King sat on a lavatory with his trousers round his ankles, and a loosely rolled cigarette between his lips.

It better be good, he said. It better be fucking brilliant. Or I fuck you up your tight Paki ass.

Two Wh'appen? shirts, one on each side, twisted his arms behind his back and forced him on to his knees, his head down between the King's knees. He gasped.

What's that? the King said. You going to have to speak up, baby boy.

The Wh'appen? shirts twisted his arms a bit more.

I can't hear you, the King said. What you say?

He groaned, and the Wh'appen? shirts twisted again.

Speak up, boy, the King said.

He shouted with pain, and they let his arms go. The King clamped his head between his knees.

That's better, he said. I like to hear when people speak to me. Now look up and tell me about this idea you got.

The King clamped his knees tighter.

Come on, boy, he said. Look up. Look me in the eyes, boy.

He dragged his head free, and looked up into the King's face.

See the whites of my eyes, boy, the King said. Come closer.

One of the Wh'appen? shirts put his foot on his back and pushed him forward. His cheek pressed against the King's stomach, the stench of the King's shit rising from the bowl under his nose, he told the King his idea.

It would make the King money, he said. He was a good cook, he said. Every day now he brought the ingredients and he and Junior Senior cooked them after school. He could make cakes, and biscuits, and pies, and whatever, and the King could sell them. It could make the King rich, he said.

The King said nothing for a long time. He could hear the King's stomach rumbling under his ear.

I'm rich already, the King said.

Richer, he said.

Where you get all this stuff from? the King said.

Home, he said.

Home, huh? the King said. Some home, huh? Some rich home. You got money to burn, man?

I can manage it, he said.

The King was silent again.

I want your money, he said finally, what's to stop me just taking it? Why bother with all this cake and biscuit shit?

More money, he said. People will pay more than the ingredients cost. I can do them very well. I've just invented a new sort of doughnut.

OK, the King said. You convinced me. Now: what's in it for you?

You get them to leave me alone, he said. You've got the power. They listen to you.

They don't, they're in deep shit, the King said. What else? Nothing else, he said.

The pressure from the foot in his back increased.

No shit? the King said. All that money for something so small. Don't give me that.

There was one other thing, he said. Junior Senior. You leave him alone. He helps me. He helps me in the kitchen. You don't need him.

The pressure from the foot in his back abruptly ceased. The King as abruptly stood, and his head was forced down into the lavatory bowl.

Nice deal, baby, the King said. One thing wrong with it though. Who do you think's going to eat your muck, huh? Who you think's going to eat what your dirty Paki hands have touched?

The lavatory flushed. When his ears had cleared he slowly lifted his head out of the bowl and saw that he was alone.

He didn't see Junior Senior for a while after that. He waited that evening in the Cookery room until quarter to six, when Miss McLeod wanted to lock up, but Junior Senior didn't come. He didn't see him the next day either, or the next, and on the day after that Mr Gilbert called him into his room. He wanted to know what was going on, he said. He was worried. Well, not worried, more concerned. He was concerned about Junior Senior. Two and a half days now, and no sign of him. He had called Junior Senior's house, but either the phone was out of order, or someone simply picked it up and put it down every time he called. Did he have any idea what was going on? No? Was he sure now? He couldn't think of any reason, anything at all, why Junior Senior wouldn't come in? Yes, OK, he could be sick, but Mr Gilbert wasn't happy. Not happy at all. He wasn't totally out of touch. He did hear things, you know.

After school he went round to Junior Senior's house, but there was no answer when he knocked. Junior Senior's front door had a stained glass inset. Much of the glass was broken, and hardboard was nailed over the space. He knocked again, and rattled the letter box. He heard the phone ring inside the house. It rang twice and stopped.

When Junior Senior came back, which he did after the weekend, he was wearing the Wh'appen? sign. Their eyes met during the first lesson, but Junior Senior's flicked quickly away. He made for Junior Senior's table at the end of the lesson, but Junior Senior went straight out without looking at him. He waited in the Cookery room after school. He waited and waited. He wanted to tell Junior Senior that it was all right, that it didn't matter. But Junior Senior knew better.

Four

The mist felt like snail traces on his skin, and every few paces he stopped and rubbed his face. He held his breath for as long as he could, and when he was finally forced to gulp the air it was like inhaling cobwebs. He forced himself downwards.

Then the mist cleared, and he was in the Cookery room cutting pockets in cutlets for Veal Cordon Bleu. It was the last Cookery lesson before the Easter holiday, and Miss McLeod had arranged for them to have it in the morning, so that they could prepare and eat their final lunch. The week before they had chosen, or Miss McLeod had chosen for them, a good but not-too-complicated menu: a salad to start with, lettuce and watercress and curly endive, with goat's cheese and a vinaigrette dressing; then the Veal Cordon Bleu, with boiled rice and Parmesan; and an Apple Charlotte and cream to follow. Miss McLeod had brought in some wine. Enough for half a glass each.

He was working at the front, preparing the veal. Miss McLeod was supervising the laying of the table. If he had looked he would have seen Junior Senior on the other side of the room, helping with the Apple Charlotte. Easter was late this year. He had just changed from the black to the white Wh'appen? shirt.

When she had finished with the table Miss McLeod clapped her hands and called them all round her desk so that she could demonstrate how to prepare the veal. He listened for as long as he could, but then the mist came down again, smothering and cold; and through it came a distorted echoing sound, which he eventually recognized as his mother's voice, speaking in a language he didn't understand. And then the mist cleared again, and there he was cutting into his veal.

Miss McLeod sent them all to their places, and watched them slice cheese, mushrooms and bacon for their stuffing. Then she sent him round with the sliced veal.

Paki, they whispered as he passed. Wanker! Pouf!

When he reached Junior Senior he just stood and waited for him to take the meat. He kept his eyes on the Wh'appen? sign.

Thanks, Junior Senior said.

He moved on.

Bent cunt, they whispered. Nigger-lover! Queer!

Back at his place he started clearing away his equipment. The mist curled and bulged and pulsed at the corner of his eyes. Miss McLeod took some boys, Junior Senior among them, to the hobs to get the pans ready.

Well then, cunt, what have we got here? Farley said. A fat little Paki, he said. Haven't we then?

A fat little Paki pouf, Matthew Andrews said. A fat little Paki pouf who loves niggers.

Lost his lover, has he? Farley said. No more fingers up the Paki ass. No more black dick. I blame it on the mother, of course.

Well, you can't blame the father can you? Matthew Andrews said. He hasn't got a father to blame, has he?

What can you expect with a Paki, Farley said. I expect his Mum was getting past it. Not good enough at it to keep him. They get old quickly, Pakis.

Don't they just? Matthew Andrews said. I know one who thinks he's a man.

A man? Farley said. A man, does he! A man! Well now.

Yeah, Matthew Andrews said. What a man! A fat little Paki bent cunt man!

Junior Senior had poured oil into his pan and was running it round the base waiting for it to heat.

A man then, Farley said. Maybe he takes it like a man then?

We'll have to try him and see, Matthew Andrews said. Then he can run home to his Mum. A man, like his Dad.

They jumped back as he grabbed his knife and slashed at them. Wow! they said. Look out. There's a man loose.

He swept the knife from side to side. Farley held out his hand. Come on then, he said. Come on!

He slashed at Farley's hand and sliced it across the palm. The children were shouting by now.

Miss! they shouted. Miss! Miss!

Miss McLeod was running back from the hobs. Farley was crouching, crying, clutching his dripping hand. The mist clung to his legs, but he dodged past Miss McLeod. It dragged at his arms, but he swung the knife forward and upward into Junior Senior's stomach, and would have struck again if the tree had not brought him up short, and this time the trunk was not smooth and he could climb.

He climbed until the mist fell away and he could see over its fleecy surface to the lip of the valley where his father stood.

He waited for his father to turn. He shouted for his father to turn and see him, but his father did not turn. With one hand in his pocket and the other shielding his eyes from the sun his father stared at the horizon.

So he sat in his tree and waited, watching his father. He looked out under his hand over the mist, at his father looking out under his hand over Africa.

THE SINGLE TRACTOR TRACK

Do you remember Peggotty? Meg Moberley said from the bed.

Cecily Moberley from the window contemplated the snow-muffled garden.

Eat your breakfast, she said.

What's this in the muesli? Meg said.

Mulberries, Cecily said. Dried mulberries. I got them at Wilson and Kennard. They will make a change.

They look like spiders' eggs, Meg said. Sacks of spiders' eggs.

Will you eat it? Cecily said. Or will I change it?

Meg added milk to the muesli and stirred the mulberries out of sight.

I heard her in the night, she said. Peggotty.

The house was old and cold, and its night noises were comfortable. Floorboards snapped and joists groaned after the central heating, which they had had enough money to install only on the ground floor and which left the upper rooms as cold as a stone, switched itself off, and the fabric of the building settled. Nightly a certain stair, fourth from the bottom on the front staircase, creaked exactly twelve minutes – Meg had counted up to sixty twelve times so she knew – after Cecily had trodden on it on her way to bed. Doors and windows rattled and curtains rustled in the draughts. Sometimes, in the paddock outside Meg's window, old Peggotty snorted and kicked up her heels into a rickety canter, and Meg would be momentarily startled till she could place the noise. It was almost pleasant, lying there waiting for the adrenalin to subside, warm in the knowledge that there was nothing to fear after all.

Cecily turned from the window.

Peggotty, she said.

She walked to Meg's bed and grasped the footrail.

Peggotty, she said, has been dead for fifty years.

What difference does that make? Meg said. She woke me up. I loved Peggotty.

Cecily released the footrail, and flexed the circulation back into her hands.

So did I, she said. Eat your breakfast.

Meg Moberley was eighty-nine, and found walking difficult. Most of the day she spent in an old wicker reclining chair on the back verandah, wrapped in blankets, looking at the garden. Cecily, her sister, twelve years younger, loved gardening but felt the weight of her years too, and these days confined her efforts to the front garden, so Meg's view was pleasantly ramshackle: a downsweep of pine branches to the left, an expanse of ragged lawn backed by a tall brick wall lined with aged fruit trees, an old garage to the right, the whole for the last fortnight covered with snow. Despite the cold Meg still insisted on sitting out on her chair. She added an extra blanket, wrapped herself in coat, scarf and mittens, and kept a paraffin chimney stove burning by her side. She only left the verandah for meals, or to go to bed at night.

Meg did not enjoy bed. She found sleeping difficult. Her sense of time and whereabouts grew confused in the dark. She dreamed, and her dreams were unpleasant. Often she found it hard to know whether she was asleep or awake. Outside on the verandah, though she allowed her memories free rein, she was always in control of her thoughts, her eyes were open. In bed she lost the faculty of distinction. She could not work out what room she was in, which house she was in, how old she was. And the land of memory, so happy to roam in by day, became a sour and treacherous place. Faces she had loved grimaced at her. People, places and events she welcomed joyfully into her daylit hours changed subtly, and were polluted by fear. Meg Moberley spent much of the night afraid.

Do you remember the bat? she said.

Cecily sat on the end of the bed and smiled.

I remember, she said.

Meg raised a spoonful of muesli to her mouth, and put it down again untasted.

Don't eat it, Cecily said, if you don't want it. Just eat the toast. And drink the coffee before it gets cold.

Meg stirred the muesli.

Just leave it, Cecily said. You don't have to eat it, for God's sake.

Meg was sitting on the end of Cecily's bed when they noticed the bat. It was hanging from the curtain rail. Cecily threw back the covers and ran to the window to look at it.

It's panting, she said. It's awake. It's looking at me.

She twisted round and looked up at the bat, under her arm, her head upside-down.

How did it get in? she said.

We must let it out, Meg said. Get back into bed while I open the window.

Meg pulled down the upper sash.

It's not moving, Cecily said. It doesn't want to go.

Meg shook the curtains. The bat didn't move. Cecily jumped up and down.

It doesn't want to go, she said. It likes us.

Meg shook the curtains again. She drew the curtains right up to the bat's feet, but still it didn't move.

Get back into bed, she said. You'll catch cold.

It winked at me, Cecily said. Oh Meg, it winked at me.

Meg pulled the curtains open again, laughing.

It's hanging on one leg, Cecily said. Meg, it's moving. Catch it! Catch it!

The bat dropped from the curtain rail, and swooped round and round the room. Meg and Cecily chased after it, screaming and flapping their arms. The bat flew out of the window and away over the paddock. Meg and Cecily stood and looked after it. Cecily put her arm round Meg's waist, and Meg stroked Cecily's hair.

Oh Meg, Cecily said. Tomorrow. And tomorrow and tomorrow.

Come on, Meg said. Back to bed.

She closed the window and pulled the curtains.

Don't just lie there staring, Cecily said. Eat. Or don't eat. I can't wait all day.

I heard it, Meg said. I heard it again. It was here.

Cecily leant forward and took the breakfast tray. Meg grabbed the other side of the tray.

It was here, she said. I heard it. It frightened me.

Let go, Cecily said. Let go. You'll spill it.

She tried to lift the tray but Meg held it down.

You'll spill it, Cecily said. Let go. Meg, let go.

It frightened me, Meg said.

All right then, I will, Cecily said. Be careful. Don't pull. You'll spill it.

She let the tray go.

There, she said. I told you. You've slopped it. I told you. Sit up and I'll straighten you out.

Meg let the tray go, and Cecily took it and put it on the bedside table. She sopped up spilled milk and coffee with a napkin. She settled Meg up against the pillows, and put the tray back in her lap.

What a fuss, she said. About nothing. Nothing at all.

Meg lay rigid on her back, not daring to move. She heard the noise again, the unplaceable noise. A sort of clattering rustle. Her head and neck were stiff against the pillow, her arms taut against her sides, her eyes stretched open despite the featureless dark. Her teeth chattered and she clenched them still. She strained her ears for a repeated rustle above the flutter and thump of her blood. As she listened the bedclothes weighed against her up-turned feet, and her throbbing bunions sent pulses of pain up her legs. Gradually the pain in her legs beat into time with the blood in her ears, and her body felt as if it was rocking on the mattress. Against her will the rocking lulled her. Slowly her limbs untensed. Cautiously she moved her arm towards her bedside light. The table was much closer than she thought, and she stubbed her fingers on it. She heard the rustle again and sleep abruptly overtook her. When she awoke some hours later, to a still-dark midwinter room with sounds of morning beyond the curtains, the fear, though milder, was still with her. It took her several minutes to realize that she was not where she had thought herself, that the old companionably noisy house was long sold, Peggotty long dead, and the bat a happy memory. She lay dozing till Cecily roused her for breakfast.

Nothing at all, Cecily said. Now please eat something. I have to get on.

Meg took a sip of coffee. There was a rustling sound and she froze with the cup to her lips.

There, she said. It's here. I told you.

Cecily stood up and listened.

I told you, Meg said.

Shh! Cecily said. Quiet!

It's here, Meg said.

Give me the cup, Cecily said.

She took the coffee cup and put it on the saucer. There was another rustle.

Cecily, Meg said. Find it. It's here.

Quiet, Cecily said. Quiet. Don't be silly. I'll find it. Wait. When it comes again I'll find it.

They waited. Another rustle, and Meg pointed to the fireplace.

It's there, she said. Behind the screen. It came down the chimney.

Cecily went to the fireplace.

Shh! she said. You'll frighten it.

Gently she moved the firescreen, and a pigeon flew, clattering and scattering soot, out of the grate. Meg shrieked, The bat! The bat! and dragged the bedclothes over her head, sending the tray and its contents flying across the room. Cecily opened the window. The bird swooped round and round the room and she chased it flapping her arms, while Meg blubbered and wailed beneath the bedclothes. The bird flew out of the window, dashing Cecily's face with its wing as it passed. Cecily closed the window, and leaned panting against the wall.

It's all right, she said. It's gone. It's only a bird. A pigeon.

Meg lay still and silent.

Meg, Cecily said. It's gone. Meg.

She went to the bed and prodded Meg's shrouded form.

THE SINGLE TRACTOR TRACK

Meg, she said. Meg. It's gone. It was only a bird. Meg.

She pulled back the bedclothes. Meg sat bolt upright, covered her face with her hands, and screamed.

Stop it, Cecily said. Stop it. It's all right.

She pulled Meg's hands away from her face. Meg screamed and screamed.

Meg, Cecily said. Stop it.

Meg struggled to free her hands, and screamed again. She tugged against Cecily's grip, and they fought. Eventually Cecily was able to hold both of Meg's hands in one of hers, and slapped her twice, very hard, across the face with the other.

Stop it! she said. Stop it!

Meg took a deep breath and was quiet.

Quiet, Cecily said. Quiet.

You've got soot, Meg said, all over your face.

Cecily hugged Meg, rocked her back and forth, and stroked her hair.

Oh Meg, she said. Tomorrow. And tomorrow and tomorrow.

What finally drove her out was Brenda's phone call. The snow had stopped at eleven, and the kids had whined to go out, but there was the tree to be decorated, and then lunch, and she hadn't allowed them. Brenda was the next-door neighbour. At least, she lived in the maisonette above the flat next door. Sometimes she stood on her balcony, and shouted greetings down to Peggy, but the snow had stopped her doing that this morning. She and Peggy had been neighbours for years. But Peggy had been virtually unaware of her until, sometime during the summer, something had happened, and suddenly wherever she looked there was Brenda. She started playing France Inter at full volume on the balcony, and shouting things like *Patience! je prends mon bain*. She was not French. Peggy was driven from her bedroom – which overlooked the garden, and where she liked to spend the afternoon lying in bed reading after she had packed the kids off to play in the park – by the noise. Then things began to drop from the balcony: shirts, tea-towels, a brassière, that Brenda had pegged out

136

to dry, and Brenda would appear at the edge and yodel for their return. After that it wasn't long before she started knocking at the door and telephoning. Peggy found it hard to bear.

Today she telephoned at half past one, just after the kids had finally settled in front of the television and Peggy was enjoying a quiet cigarette in the kitchen before tackling the washing up.

Hi! she said. Hi! How are you? How are the kids? Listen, you must come over for a Christmas drink some time. What are you doing this afternoon? Why not come over? I don't feel a bit christmassy, do you? Oh, Christmas isn't what it was. But nothing ever is, is it? What it was.

I'm sorry, Peggy said. I can't. But I promised the kids. We're getting out. You just caught me actually.

Oh well, Brenda said. Tonight then. Come over tonight. I tell you what. Why don't I come and see you? Get the kids in bed in time for Santa Claus and we can have a chat and get tipsy. How about it?

OK, Peggy said. OK, why not? I'll see you this evening then.

Right, Brenda said. I wish I felt christmassy, but I don't. Not even with all the snow. Maybe I will tonight. See you then.

See you, Peggy said.

She put down the receiver, and gritted her teeth.

William! she called. Susan! Put your coats on. We're going out.

They didn't want to go, of course. All morning fussing and fretting to go out, and now they had the opportunity they'd rather watch television. So she went into the sitting room and turned the set off.

Get your fucking coats on, and get into the fucking car, she said. We are going for a drive.

Brenda tapped on the window and waved as they went down to the car. William and Susan ignored her and climbed silently into the back seat. Peggy waited for Brenda to tap again before she looked up, smilingly cursed, and waved back. She slammed the door, savagely revved the engine, and took two corners very fast. Then she stopped and turned to face the tribunal in the back seat.

Sorry, she said.

Why do you see her, William said. If you don't like her?

Good question, Peggy said.

She smiles, Susan said. All the time. All the time.

When you live alone for a long time, Peggy said, you get a bit strange.

You live alone, Susan said.

I know I swore at you, Peggy said. But you're not going to walk out on me, are you?

Not that sort of alone, William said. She hasn't got a husband or anything.

That's all right, Susan said. I swear sometimes too.

It helps, Peggy said.

It's Christmas, William said. Everybody's supposed to be nice at Christmas.

I'm sorry, Peggy said.

No, Susan said. Not that. He means that's why you're nice to her. It's Christmas.

Well, Peggy said. Thanks.

But, William said.

I know, Peggy said. I'm a coward. I should tell her.

To fuck off, Susan said.

I'm afraid that's what it would have to be, Peggy said. She wouldn't understand anything less.

I'll tell her for you, Susan said.

Don't you know anything? William said. You never tell anyone to fuck off when you really mean it. Isn't that right?

Peggy clambered round and knelt on the seat. She leaned over and hugged William and kissed him. Then Susan.

William sniffed and sat back in the furthest corner of the car.

All right, all right, he said.

Susan kissed her mother's cheek.

Yes, Peggy said. Yes. Where shall we go?

Cobb's Hill, Susan said.

Immediately William came back out of his corner and suggested Longleat. For a while they bickered energetically: We always go where you want to go. No we don't, we went where you wanted last time. In the end, slowly because of the snowpacked roads, Peggy just drove. When it became obvious that neither Longleat nor Cobb's Hill was their destination, both children sulked. Peggy took the Dorset road out of town, and headed over the Downs. The sky was grey and flurries of snow fell. Soon William took his latest game out of his pocket, and they started to play. It wasn't a quiet game, and it didn't take Peggy long to bow out.

It's too difficult, she said. I can't play and drive in this weather. Just carry on without me. I'll be all right.

Half a mile outside Hindon the engine started tucking and Peggy decided to turn back. In the middle of her three-point turn it stopped altogether and nothing would persuade it to start again.

William span the wheel. What L is your favourite tree? he said.

Lime tree, Susan said. Lime tree.

That doesn't count, William said. It's not your favourite. You don't even know what it looks like.

So what, Susan said. That's not the point. It's just any tree. It doesn't have to be your favourite.

Yes it does, William said. Of course it does. I'm going to spin again.

Mummy, Susan said. William's cheating. Just because he didn't win.

I'm not cheating, William said. You're the cheat. Lime tree!

Has it struck you, Peggy said, that we have stopped half-way across the road, and it may snow again any minute?

We didn't want to come anyway, William said.

Peggy clenched the steering wheel.

If, she said, you are not out of this car and pushing in ten seconds flat I shall take your Christmas present, when and if we get home, and burn it.

The children got out and pushed from behind, while Peggy pushed from the side and steered at the same time. Jumping into the car again just in time to put on the brake, Peggy barked her knee on the door and tore her tights. The children got back into the car.

Settling in, are we? Peggy said. Keeping warm while Mummy goes for help? Not likely. Out. We've got a telephone to find.

It's cold, Susan said.

Yes, Peggy said. Isn't it?

Where are we going? William said.

Into the unknown, Peggy said. Follow me and no straggling. The enemy always picks off the last one.

Keep together, Susan said. Our lives may depend on it.

Silly, William said. It's no good pretending it's fun. It's bloody awful, and you know it, and it's your fault.

He stomped off towards Hindon, and Peggy and Susan followed.

Bloody awful, he said. Come on!

After lunch it snowed again. Not much. Just enough to cover the bird tracks on the lawn. Meg Moberley lay on her chair and watched them vanish. She had always had good eyes. No matter what Cecily may say, she had seen the airship.

Cecily! she called. Cecily!

On the crown of Cobb's Hill, inside the ring of fortifications, she lay on her back and stared straight up into the void to rest her eyes. The grass was densely packed and springy as horsehair. A slight wind blew over the surrounding ramparts, not even strong enough to ruffle the pages of her sketchpad, but cool on the skin.

Meg! Cecily called. Meg!

Meg held her arm up in front of her eyes, and twisted it this way and that, noting with satisfaction its honey colour and firmly muscled contours. Short and capable hands, she thought. Not pretty, not graceful, though in an honest sort of way beautiful. Strong and square. Working hands. Sturdily knuckled. Fingers smudged with charcoal and calloused from gripping pencil and brush. The nails bitten short and neat.

Meg! Cecily called.

At what point, Meg wondered, did a painterly interest in one's own structure turn into a mirror-gazing self-absorption? She sat up and hugged her knees.

Here, she called. Cecily, here.

Cecily, in pinafore and plaits, appeared on the ramparts.

Yes, she said. What is it?

I saw it, Meg said. I did see it.

What? Cecily said. What did you see?

She picked up the sketchpad.

What have you been doing? she said.

Just an idea, Meg said. I thought I'd do a big canvas. Just a sketch. From up there.

Let me see, Cecily said.

She took the sketchpad up on to the rampart, and walked round the crown of the hill, checking the drawing against the view.

Here, she said.

Meg stood up and joined her. Cecily looked at the drawing again, and out over the fields that stretched towards Bristol.

You did it from here, she said. The clouds have changed a bit, but otherwise it's just the same.

Except for this, she said. What's this? I can't see it.

Let me look, Meg said. What?

This, Cecily said. This bit. It looks like a fleck, or a cross, or something.

She pointed over the fields.

It isn't there, she said. I don't see why you put it in. It isn't there.

Meg looked at the pad, and the view.

Of course it is, she said. Look.

I'm looking, Cecily said. It isn't there.

Don't be silly, Meg said. Of course it is.

Again Meg looked. Tiny, silent, bright, the airship floated above Bristol.

Maybe it was a bird or something, Cecily said. And now it's gone.

Meg snatched the sketchpad from her, closed it, and hugged it to her chest.

Nonsense, she said. You're just not looking.

141

Now who's being silly? Cecily said. I call it pretty silly, insisting something's there when it plainly isn't.

But it's there, she said. I can see it.

She shivered, and huddled deeper into her pile of coats and blankets. She rubbed her gloved hands together, and moaned.

I did see it, she said. Why don't you believe me?

What? Cecily said. What is it? What did you see?

The airship, Meg said. It was there.

For God's sake, Cecily said. What on earth are you talking about?

I'm cold, Meg said.

Of course you're cold, Cecily said. What do you expect, sitting out here in the worst winter for years.

Move the stove closer, Meg said.

It's too close anyway, Cecily said. You'll burn the place to the ground one day.

I did see it, Meg said.

Yes, Cecily said. I expect you did. Of course you did. Come on. I'll tidy up your blankets. They're all untucked.

Then why did you say it wasn't there? Meg said.

Briskly Cecily straightened and tucked the blankets.

Why? Meg said.

Meg, Cecily said, I'm trying to be patient. I am trying very hard not to scream. Will you please be quiet?

I don't understand, Meg said. Why say you didn't see it, when you did? When it was so beautiful.

Slowly, slowly, the airship turned and shone over the distant sparkle of the Bristol Channel. The doorbell shrilled. Both sisters jumped.

Just lie still, Cecily said. Who can that be? Lie still and rest. I'll be back soon.

Meg and Cecily walked hand in hand down Cobb's Hill. At the bottom they broke into a run.

Race you, Meg said.

They ran to the car. Cecily won. They climbed panting into their seats, and Meg started the engine.

Vroom tuck-a tuck-a tuck-a.

Meg pulled the starter again but the engine just turned over and stopped.

Try it again, Meg's father said.

Vroom tuck-a tuck-a tuck.

She stood up and looked over the tractor's bonnet. All she could see of her father was his upturned feet, wearing an old pair of embroidered Turkish slippers, as he tinkered under the old Allis Chalmers' belly.

Try it again, he said.

Meg looked at her father's feet and laughed.

Do you always wear your slippers in the yard? she said.

Try the engine, her father said. I wear what I like. When I like.

Meg sat down again and pulled the starter. This time the engine started.

Vroom tuck-a tuck-a tuck-a.

Oh Susan, Meg's father said. You've spoiled it.

I can't help it, the girl said. You go too fast.

Come on then, the boy said. Stay level with me. Ready?

Ready, the girl said.

Vroom tuck-a tuck-a tuck-a, the boy said. Oh hello.

Hello, Meg said.

The girl put her hand to her mouth and said nothing.

My name's William, the boy said. And this is my sister Susan. We're playing tractors.

You're doing it very well, Meg said. I thought you were a real one. I used to drive tractors sometimes.

She's not very good, William said. She gets left behind.

Susan smiled at Meg and looked down at her feet.

You go too fast, she said. My feet get tangled up.

What you do, William said, is this. You walk with your feet like this.

He demonstrated.

It leaves a track, he said, like tractor tyres. In the snow.

Yes, Meg said. I can see it does. How clever.

Of course it only works with two, William said. You can't do it by yourself.

No, Meg said. I can see that.

Susan sniffed.

It's not fair, she said. He's bigger than me. He goes too fast.

Why don't you try again, Meg said. Wheel round and come up here. We could sit and talk.

I don't want to, Susan said.

That's a pity, Meg said. I should like to see you do it.

Spoilsport, William said.

I don't care, Susan said. I'm cold and I want to go home. My gloves are wet.

So are mine, William said. I'm not complaining.

I've got a heater up here, Meg said.

All right, Susan said. Come on then.

Vroom tuck-a tuck-a tuck-a, William said.

Carefully in time they placed the heel of one foot against the arch of the other and left parallel tractor tracks across the lawn and up to the foot of the verandah. William twisted his hand in front of him as if turning a key.

Chug chug, he said. There.

Meg held out her hands.

Very good, she said. Come on up. Give me your gloves.

The children gave her their gloves and sat on the top step.

They are very wet aren't they? Meg said. I'd better put them on the stove.

She waved the gloves at the stove, and William, seeing that she couldn't reach, got up and moved it towards her.

Just spread them on top, Meg said. They'll soon be warm and dry.

Thank you, William said.

Well, Meg said. I must say it's nice to have visitors. We don't see many people, you know. Not now.

Our car broke down, Susan said. And we had to walk. We knocked on your door.

I think Mummy's telephoning, William said. The other lady said she could.

144

We're a long way from home, Susan said. I hope we get back all right.

Of course we will, William said.

I don't want to have Christmas here, Susan said.

Susan! William said. Don't be rude. This lady lives here.

Well I don't, Susan said.

It won't be long, William said. Mummy will phone the AA. We'll be home in an hour.

I used to drive tractors, Meg said. For my father sometimes.

Her honey-coloured tight-muscled forearm clenched as she gripped the steering wheel. Father held on behind. She opened the throttle.

Faster! Cecily shouted. Faster!

Cecily sat on her knee as she drove. The wind rushed in her face. It was difficult to breathe.

Let me, Cecily shouted. Let me.

Better not, Father said.

I want to, Cecily said. I want to steer.

No, Father said. Better not. You'd have us in the bank. We'd end up in the bank.

Poor Cecily. She could never understand why just by putting her hand on the steering wheel she would transport them five miles away into town and into the Bank.

I want to, she said. I want to.

Meg pushed the tractor as fast as it would go, and laughed into the wind.

Twenty-five miles an hour, Father said.

No.

Wait.

That can't be right. I'm getting mixed up. We didn't have a tractor then. There weren't any tractors then. When Cecily was that young.

The wind blew in her face.

He meant the bank at the side of the road, of course, Meg said.

I'm sorry, William said. What?

Not the Bank, Meg said.

145

I wear what I want, Father said. If I want to drive in slippers I shall drive in slippers. You can get down now. I'll take over.

What bank? William said.

Meg got off the tractor.

I should like to drive, she said.

I'm sure you would, Father said.

Meg stood and watched as he drove away.

Slippers, Meg said.

What slippers? William said. Where? Do you want me to fetch them for you?

I think she's asleep, Susan said. Or something. She's dreaming.

Faster! Cecily shouted. Faster!

I want to go home, Susan said.

Father drove away. All that was left of the tractor was a dying noise, vroom tuck-a tuck-a tuck-a, and the smell of exhaust.

The room was virtually bare except for the pictures. Indeed, Peggy saw as she sat on the only chair to telephone the AA, there wouldn't have been room for much else. Every available inch of wall was covered, and there were more, stacked five or six deep, under the window and in the corners, and in a sort of pyramid in the middle of the room. Enough, she thought, to give you vertigo, or at least a lousy headache, in a very short time. Certainly too many for you to form any idea of their quality. Or even their content. All you could see, all you could feel, was gusts and waves of colour. She looked out of the window, to where the kids were playing some sort of footprint game in the snow, and dialled. A man, they said, would be out from Shaftesbury in about an hour. Merry Christmas!

Miss Moberley knocked on the door and came in with a cup of tea.

Oh, you've finished, she said. I've brought you this, but I expect you'd rather have it in the drawing room.

Thanks, Peggy said. It's a bit overpowering in here.

I don't come in very often, Miss Moberley said. The pictures are my sister's. I have a telephone by my bed.

Peggy shut the door on the pictures with relief, and followed Miss Moberley into a drawing room mercifully restful to the eye.

Over the years I have come to hate them, Miss Moberley said. For one reason or another. As I say, they are my sister's. Is your tea all right?

Perfect, Peggy said.

You wouldn't like sugar, or maybe a sherry, or something, Miss Moberley said.

Tea's fine, Peggy said.

My sister is older than I, Miss Moberley said. And more or less bedridden. She hasn't painted for some time. Or looked at her pictures. But she won't let them go. It's rather difficult really.

I mustn't stay long, Peggy said. They said they'd only be an hour. And it'll take half an hour at least to get back to the car.

Twelve years older, Miss Moberley said. We used to be friends. We used to love each other. But twelve years is a big difference now we're old.

I suppose it must be, Peggy said.

How old are your children? Miss Moberley said.

Seven and eight, Peggy said.

Ah yes, Miss Moberley said. It makes a difference when they're that close. When I was seven or eight she was so grown up. And now she's so old. More tea?

No, Peggy said. No thanks. I think I'd better be going. You've been very kind.

Cruel really, Miss Moberley said.

I'm sorry, Peggy said.

It's cruel, Miss Moberley said. To be so old. It makes a nonsense of all the time in between. When we were friends.

Yes, Peggy said. I suppose it does.

Well, Miss Moberley said. If you must, you must.

I really should, Peggy said.

I'll see you to the door, Miss Moberley said.

At the front door Peggy shook Miss Moberley's hand.

Thank you again, she said. I wonder where the children are. They must have gone round the back.

I hope not, Miss Moberley said.

I expect they have, Peggy said. I'm sorry. I didn't know they weren't supposed to.

I suppose it's natural that they should, Miss Moberley said. It doesn't matter. You'd better call them.

William! Peggy shouted. Susan! We're going!

She took a few paces into the garden and called again. She turned and smiled at Miss Moberley, who did not smile in return. She shrugged and was about to call for a third time when she was prevented by a long gurgling scream.

Miss Moberley said Christ! and turned and sped into the house. Peggy followed her through the hall and a large bare kitchen on to a verandah at the back of the house. William and Susan were huddled together at one end of the verandah, and at the other an old lady lay screaming on a reclining chair. Beyond her lay an overturned paraffin heater, pouring smoke. Miss Moberley stood in the middle of the verandah, staring at the smoke.

For God's sake, Peggy said. Do something. She'll burn.

The old woman lay under a pile of blankets and coats. Peggy snatched the top one of these, an old duffle coat, and smothered the burning heater.

Thank you, Miss Moberley said.

What happened? Peggy said.

My gloves, William said.

We put them on the stove to dry, Susan said. Mine too.

And then they started to burn, William said. And when we tried to take them off, we knocked it over.

You? Miss Moberley said. You?

Yes, Susan said.

You're sure? Miss Moberley said. You're sure it was you?

Me actually, William said.

I see, Miss Moberley said.

She turned to the old woman on the reclining chair, whose screams gave way to silent mouthings and gulps for air.

Is this true, she said.

I'm sure it is, Peggy said. William, you are very stupid and very naughty. You've caused a lot of trouble.

Miss Moberley went to the old woman and put her hand on her shoulder.

Is this true? she said.

The old woman sobbed.

It's true, she said. Don't hit me. It wasn't my fault.

I think we'd better go, Peggy said. Come on you two. Your hands will freeze, and serve you right.

I don't believe you, Miss Moberley said. You coward. To hide behind children.

I'm sorry, Peggy said. But if William says he did it, I believe him.

I'm sorry too, Miss Moberley said. You're right. You'd better go.

Will you be all right? Peggy said.

Oh yes, Miss Moberley said. We'll be all right. We can cope. You can go.

Peggy took the children and went. When they were at the gate, Miss Moberley called after them.

Wait, she called. Wait.

She hurried down the garden path, carrying a large oil painting.

I'd like you to have this, she said.

I couldn't, Peggy said. Really I couldn't.

I'd like you to have it, Miss Moberley said. I'm sorry. I was rude. Please take it.

I really couldn't, Peggy said.

Please, Miss Moberley said. After all, we don't need them. We never look at them. Please.

She held out the picture.

Please, she said. A Christmas present.

You're very kind, Peggy said.

A Christmas present, Miss Moberley said. She could have burned. My sister could have burned.

Peggy took the picture.

Well, she said. Thank you. You're very kind.

Happy Christmas, Miss Moberley said.

It started to snow on their way back to the car. By the time the AA man came it was falling heavily. Peggy and the kids sat in the car and waited while he fixed the engine. The oil painting was propped up on the front seat.

Should be all right now, the AA man said. Just a blocked fuel pipe. Have you got far to go?

Not far, Peggy said. To Warminster.

You'll be all right, the AA man said. Take longer in this weather though.

Driving across the Downs, Peggy glanced back at the kids in the mirror.

Was it really you? she said.

I said it was, William said. Didn't I?

Oh yes, Peggy said. You did. I just wondered.

Well then, William said.

OK, forget it, Peggy said.

Is it a nice picture? Susan said.

I haven't really looked at it, Peggy said.

She didn't like it, Susan said. She said so. More or less.

She didn't like the old lady either, William said. I did. I thought she was nice. We talked about tractors.

Why didn't she like her? Susan said.

It's hard, Peggy said. Sometimes when two people have lived together for a long time.

Yes? William said.

They get, Peggy said.

They get what? William said. What do they get?

Oh God, Peggy said. I don't know. Why must I always have all the answers?

Cecily Moberley closed the Aga door, and went to the sink to wash up pans and chopping boards. The light from the kitchen shone over the verandah and a wedge of lawn. Out of the light, on the edge of the verandah, Meg lay on her chair. Beside her the heater, charred but still working, glowed in the dark. It had stopped snowing. All she could see of Meg was her muffled silhouette. She opened the window.

Finished, she said. We can eat in an hour.

Meg said nothing. Cecily closed the window, and went to the dining room. After she'd laid the table, she put the sherry decanter and two glasses on to a tray, and carried them out to the verandah.

I thought we could have a drink, she said. How beautiful the snow looks. Fresh fallen snow.

Meg still said nothing. Cecily balanced the tray on the verandah rail, and poured two glasses. Her back to Meg, she looked out at the snow.

Clean and white, she said. Meg, I'm trying to say I'm sorry. For everything. For being younger than you.

She turned round and held out a glass.

Have a drink, she said. With me. The two of us.

Meg fumbled at her blankets.

Meg, Cecily said. Meg. For the past. For all the years.

Meg threw off one blanket, then another.

Listen, Cecily said. Listen to me. What are you doing?

Meg swung her legs off the chair, and heaved herself to her feet. Her arms held out to keep her balance, she lurched to the edge of the verandah. Cecily took a step towards her.

No, Meg said. No.

She stepped heavily down the stairs and on to the lawn. Carefully she placed the heel of one foot against the arch of the other, and moved, unsteadily at first, then with more confidence, across the snow, into the dark.

Cecily put the sherry glasses back on the tray. She looked at Meg's tracks.

Vroom tuck-a tuck-a tuck-a, Meg's voice said in the darkness.

Cecily walked to the edge of the verandah and opened her mouth to call.

Vroom tuck-a tuck-a tuck-a, Meg said again.

Cecily sighed and followed her sister across the snow.

I JUST KEPT ON SMILING

We were in class. It was my birthday. I was twelve.

I hadn't told anyone it was my birthday. I try not to tell anyone anything. But at breakfast Dom Gilbert, who hands out the mail, put two large envelopes by my plate, and wished me a Happy Birthday. Everyone at my table looked at me. Dom Gilbert waited, so I smiled at him, and he went away.

I opened them after breakfast. They were cards from home. One from my father and mother. One from my elder brother. I took the cards to the art room, where we're supposed to go every morning and fill our pens, and dropped them behind the press.

It was a Latin class. What we had to do was write sentences on the board. We all had a sheet of sentences, and Dom Francis sat at the back of the room and called out names. When your name was called you went up to the blackboard, and wrote your sentence on it in Latin. If you made a mistake the others were supposed to correct you. When Dom Francis was satisfied with your version, and this could take a long time, everyone copied it into his book, and you went back to your seat.

I took the books after I'd finished my sentence. I chose my moment carefully. While everyone was copying my sentence down, and Dom Francis was looking at his list to decide who was next, I took three exercise books from the pile on his desk. I took them back to my place, slipped them into my desk, and quickly wrote my sentence.

I sit at the front of the room. I prefer it that way.

At the end of the lesson Dom Francis collected in our books, and cleared his desk into his bag. Three was just the right number of exercise books to have taken. He wouldn't notice they were gone till he counted the pile.

After lunch we have half an hour to ourselves, before Games. We're meant to spend it in the day room. I like to spend it in the Chapel. If people ask where you've been, and you say the

Chapel, they think you're a bit odd, but they don't say anything. The Chapel has a big gallery at the back where nobody ever sits except parents on Visitors' Day. I go there whenever I can, which isn't often, because I'm no fool. You can't keep a place if you go there too often. People nose you out. I go there once or twice a week maybe.

So after lunch I went back to the classroom, took the books from my desk, put them under my pullover – carefully, because I didn't want to crease them – and took them to the Chapel.

They were beautiful. Clean, stiff, and empty. When I opened them they crackled.

I held them by the edge. My hands are sweaty, and I didn't want to mark them.

I decided to keep them in the old vestment chest at the back of the gallery. It's full of old copes and chasubles and things that aren't used any more. No one ever goes to it. It isn't even locked. I put the exercise books right at the bottom, and rearranged the vestments on top of them.

On the way down from the Chapel I met Nicky Carver. He said Hello, How are you, Happy Birthday. I smiled at him. I have a good smile. It makes people think twice.

Nicky Carver and I are about equal. He sits just behind me in class. His bed is opposite mine in the dormitory. We are about the same level in class. People usually bracket Nicky Carver and me together.

He walked with me to the changing room where we got ready for Games. I think he likes Games as little as I do, but there isn't any point in complaining.

The next time we saw Dom Francis was the last lesson before supper that evening. We all stood up when he came in, and said Good evening, Dom Francis. He said nothing.

He went to his desk and stood facing us. He looked at us all in turn. Behind me I could hear shifting feet. When it was my turn to be looked at I stared at the space between his eyes. He sat down.

I have bad news, he said. There is a thief among us. No one will sit down till he owns up.

I was still looking at the space between his eyes.

Well, he said. I'm waiting.

Nobody said anything.

This morning, he said, when I came to this class, I had twenty seven exercise books. When I left I had twenty-four. Who can explain this?

He looked at us all in turn again. I looked at the bridge of his nose.

Very well, he said. I will give the thief a chance to redeem himself. My study will be open all tomorrow morning. I shall not be there. If, by twelve o'clock, the three exercise books are on my desk, I will consider the matter closed. Meanwhile, perhaps half an hour on your feet will improve your powers of concentration.

We stood for the rest of the lesson, and did Greek irregular verbs.

We had some time to ourselves again after supper. I spent it in the day room with Nicky Carver, playing chess. We discussed the rest of the class, and Nicky Carver tried to work out who had taken the exercise books. Nicky Carver is very religious. He has a brother in Rome, training to be a priest.

At lunch the next day Dom Francis rang the bell for silence and announced that he wanted to see all our class immediately afterwards in his study.

We formed a line outside his door, and Nicky Carver stood next to me.

When Dom Francis arrived he called us all in together and invited us to look at his desk.

As you can see, he said, the exercise books have not been returned. I must therefore punish the whole class.

Michael Byrne and Christopher Wynne-Wilson burst into tears. They often do.

What anyone, Dom Francis said, would want with three school exercise books is beyond me. I mean what possible use could there be for them? Be quiet, you two.

Michael Byrne and Christopher Wynne-Wilson managed to stop crying.

I apologize, Dom Francis said, in advance to those of you whom I must punish unjustly. To those of you who did not steal the books, and do not know who did. You must all understand that I have no choice. I shall see you all here at this time tomorrow, and I shall beat you all.

This time Anthony Forde joined Michael Byrne and Christopher Wynne-Wilson. Dom Francis looked at us as they cried.

Of course, he said, there is still time for the culprit to own up. And save his friends. I hope he does. Now go to Games.

After Games Anthony Forde, Timothy Pigott and Freddy Oake came up to me in the changing room. Freddy Oake punched my arm. He often does.

Forde, he said, has got something to say to you. Tell him, Forde.

I saw you, Anthony Forde said. I saw you take them.

No, you didn't, I said. When was that?

At the end of the lesson, he said. Just before Dom Francis left. While he was collecting in our books. You leaned forward and took them off his desk.

So where are they now, I said.

Who knows? Freddy Oake said.

He punched my arm again.

And who cares? he said.

All we know, Timothy Pigott said, is that you're going to own up to Dom Francis.

They pushed me down on to the floor, Timothy Pigott sat on my chest and pulled my tie very tight round my throat.

You are going to tell Dom Francis, he said. Aren't you?

Yes, I said. Yes.

He let my tie go.

Aren't you? he said.

Yes, I said. I told you.

As I said before, I'm no fool. I know Timothy Pigott.

He got off my chest, and I sat up. They stood round me.

Just remember, Freddy Oake said. That's all.

Then they all kicked me, and went away. I finished changing.

After supper I went and spent some time in the Chapel. I didn't look at the exercise books. I didn't even go up into the gallery.

Nicky Carver came up to me in the dormitory that night.

I heard, he said. I don't think you should do it.

I smiled at him, but he didn't go away.

It's wrong, he said.

You know Pigott, I said.

So we all get beaten, he said. I don't think you should do it. It's wrong.

Never mind, I said. Quite a lot of things are wrong. Like taking the books in the first place.

It would be all right, he said, if you were doing it for us. But you're not. You're doing it because you're afraid of Pigott.

You bet I am, I said. Of course I am. Aren't you?

That's not the point, he said. I don't think you should do it.

We had Dom Francis again the second lesson next morning. We all stood behind our chairs. He sat down and told us to sit, and I stayed standing. He looked at me and I stared between his eyes.

The exercise books, I said. It was me. I took them.

Thank you, he said, for telling me. Come and see me at the end of the lesson.

He set us an unseen. I felt him looking at me about half-way through the lesson. I looked up and smiled, and he turned away.

After the others had left he called me up to his desk.

Well, he said. So it was you.

Yes sir, I said.

You are the thief, he said.

Yes sir, I said.

He sighed.

Who put you up to this? he said.

I don't know what you mean sir, I said. I'm owning up. I took them.

He brought his fist down hard on the desk.

Do you take me for a total fool? he said. Tell me who made you do this.

I'm sorry sir, I said. It's true. I did take them.

159

Then where are they? he said. Take me to them.

I didn't say anything.

Come on, he said. I'm waiting. Where are they?

I looked between his eyes, and then down at my feet.

I thought so, he said. Are you going to tell me who made you do it?

I'm sorry sir, I said. I don't know what you mean.

Get out, he said. Go away and tell your friends that they'll have to get up a lot earlier in the morning if they want to fool me. Go on. Get out.

Nicky Carver was waiting for me outside.

He didn't believe me, I said.

Good, he said.

At lunch Dom Francis rang the bell for silence again, and said we were all to see him in his study afterwards.

He stood us in rows in front of his table.

*I'm sure you all know, he said, of this morning's disgraceful episode. So I will say no more about it. It has changed nothing. We must all resign ourselves to the knowledge that there is a thief in our midst. I don't know how he will live with his shame. He has stolen. He has betrayed his friends. There are parents, and members of staff, who are non-Catholics, or who have recently converted. What will they think of us now? You will all line up outside, and come in one by one for your punishment. Then you will wait outside till I dismiss you.

We lined up outside. I was near the end of the line. We counted eight strokes each. Michael Byrne and Christopher Wynne-Wilson cried. I was very careful not to look at Timothy Pigott. When it came to my turn, Dom Francis was red in the face and out of breath. His hair was all over the place.

I took down my trousers and bent over his chair and took my eight strokes. Dom Francis beats you with an old leather slipper.

Afterwards he held out his hand and I shook it.

You must see, he said, that I have no choice.

Yes, sir, I said. Thank you sir.

When he'd beaten us all he called us all back in.

The incident is now closed, he said. I want you all to be very clear on this. Especially those of you who are responsible for this morning's misguided little charade, for which I have given you all two extra strokes. The matter will not be discussed again. I will punish any boy who does so.

Shame, I said to Nick Carver as we were changing for Games. What does he know about shame?

We're not supposed to talk about it, Nicky Carver said.

I avoided Timothy Pigott as far as I could, in case his sense of honour was not as keen as Nicky Carver's. He left me alone. Perhaps two extra strokes were enough for him. Perhaps he didn't care now that it was all over. Anthony Forde tried to speak to me that night after supper, but I just smiled at him and looked away.

I didn't go to the Chapel for a week. I spent my free time in the day room with the rest. Sometimes I played chess with Nicky Carver. Most of the time I sat and read.

I thought of the exercise books often. How clean and white they were. How empty. Thinking about them helped me a lot. At the end of that week I went to the Chapel and looked at them. They smelled of incense from the vestments. I looked at them once or twice a week from then on.

I saw more of Nicky Carver. We went on walks together, and he told me about his home. He lives near Manchester. Exeat day came round, and his parents came down to visit him, and mine came to visit me. They met, and they talked, and we went out to tea.

His parents asked mine if I would like to go and stay with them during the holidays, and mine said that I would. They didn't ask me.

That evening I decided to tear up the exercise books and throw them away. I went to the Chapel after supper to get them, and took them to the lavatory. I tore them up into minute pieces and flushed them away. It took a long time. I thought I might keep a small piece to remind me of them but in the end I didn't.

I didn't need to be reminded of anything. I had a secret.

My mother wrote to me and said that she and Mrs Carver had

arranged that I was to spend a week with them after Easter. She was glad I had a friend, she said.

That evening I took Freddy Oake's tennis eye-shade, which I'd had my eye on for some time. He'd left it in the recess between the small Library and the second form classroom, and I took it after supper.

I went to the Chapel to inspect it, and sat looking at it for a long time. It was a cool crescent of shining green plastic. But it didn't have the magic of the exercise books. In fact I thought it might get in the way of their memory. So I decided to put it back.

I bumped into Nicky Carver on the way back to the recess. The eye-shade was under my pullover. He stayed with me and talked. About his home, and the woods near his home, where we'd walk when I came to stay. He came with me back to the small Library, and I slipped the eye-shade back into the recess.

He must have seen me do it. I caught him looking at me very oddly in the dormitory later. We were sitting up in our beds waiting for lights-out. He just stared at me. I smiled at him, but he didn't stop. He just stared and stared till Dom Gilbert put out the light.

Before lunch the next day we were all lined up in the hall ready to go to lunch when Dom Francis came in to make an announcement. He called Nicky Carver out and told him to go and wait in his study. Then he spoke to us.

Some of you will remember, he said, that a few weeks ago we discovered that there was a thief among us. Not only a thief but a betrayer of his friends, as I was forced to beat his entire class because he would not own up. I said at the time that I did not know how he would live with his shame. And it seems that he cannot. He came to me this morning and confessed. You will all wait here, while I deal with him now.

Everyone stood very quiet. Dom Francis left the hall, and we all waited. I couldn't believe my ears. I could hardly breathe. I was furious. I bit my cheek I was so angry.

Dom Francis came back and told us we could go in to lunch. There was to be no talking.

Nicky Carver was standing on a table in the middle of the refectory. He was standing to attention, and there was a big placard round his neck saying, Thief.

We all went to our places and sat down. I was a server that day and had to help hand round the plates. We were all silent. When I'd finished handing round I sat down. It was so quiet the noise of my chair scraping on the floor echoed round the room. I didn't want to eat. I stared at Nicky Carver and waited for him to look my way.

It took a long time but he did in the end. I smiled at him. He had stolen my secret. He looked away.

I carried on staring, and soon he looked back at me. I smiled again. I didn't eat anything. I just kept on smiling.

FLORAL STREET

One

We are standing at the junction of Pembridge Road and the Bayswater Road, outside Notting Hill Gate Underground station, looking north. It is early morning. And winter. A man is walking towards us. He is tall, well-built almost to the point of caricature, and exactly thirty-six years old. Today is his birthday. He is wearing a Tattersall shirt, a yellow tweed tie, loose-cut green drill trousers, a maroon pullover, and brown brogues. Over this a fur-lined brown tweed overcoat, its fur collar turned up to frame his face, flaps open as he walks. His hands are in the overcoat pockets. From his right shoulder hangs a canvas fishing bag. An umbrella is crooked into his left pocket, and flaps with the coat. Under his trousers, for a variety of reasons not all of them sexual, he wears a cockring. He walks with a loose-limbed stride. Just before his face comes into focus he stops to look at the advertisement board outside the newsagent's. From the way he stands you might think he had trained as a dancer. Then again you might think his feet hurt.

That is our opening image. The scene, as it were, before the titles. Our story begins an hour earlier, and a couple of hundred yards away, in the bedroom of a largely white maisonette in Chepstow Villas. The room is beginning to lighten. Two figures, male and female, are intertwined under the duvet. Until a week ago, Martin Conrad, known to his friends as Bear, would drowse through the shipping forecast, only disentangling himself from encircling arms and forcing himself into full wakefulness to listen to the news. Lately, however, he has discontinued this practice. He finds the news depressing, and has advanced his clock radio seven minutes in order to miss it, and begin his day untrammelled by material considerations. He regards this as a great step forward. This morning, then, he is roused by Patricia Hughes's husky Good Morning Campers, and lies listening to Soler's Fandango, which he finds too interesting to clean his teeth to. When the piece is over, he pushes aside his partner's arms, pushes back the duvet, and slips out from under a pinioning thigh. His partner does not wake. He turns off the radio, and goes to the bathroom, where he inspects himself closely in the mirror, showers, cleans his teeth, moisturizes his face, and decides not to shave. He shakes his wet head, pats his hair into the most becoming tangle of curls, shakes his head again but more gently, and puts on his dressing gown. On his way from the bathroom to the stairs he pauses outside his bedroom door, lifts his hand as if to rap with his knuckles, hesitates, and puts both hands in his pockets. He says Happy birthday darling, and starts for the stairs. At the top of the stairs he draws the cockring from his pocket, and stops to put it on, frowning slightly with concentration. This done, he puts his hands back in his pockets and descends the stairs. As he descends, his belt unties and his dressing gown flaps open. He neglects to close it, and proceeds to the kitchen, where his son sits at the breakfast bar over coffee and muesli. His son inserts a spoonful of muesli into his mouth, and smiles. Martin notices that fragments of chewed grain fleck his son's teeth.

His son says, Hi dad.

Martin says, Hi kid.

His son says, Coffee's ready.

Martin pours himself a black coffee, tastes it, and grimaces.

Four years, he says. Four years since I gave up sugar, and I still hate it. They all said I'd get used to it, but I hate it.

His son stands up and walks round the breakfast bar. He hugs his father, and plants a muesli-scented kiss on his cheek.

Happy birthday Bear, he says.

Martin returns his son's hug.

Thanks kid, he says.

They sit opposite each other at the breakfast bar. Martin fills a bowl with muesli, sprinkles bran on it, adds milk, and eats.

How old are you anyway? his son says.

What have you bought me? Martin says.

I haven't bought anything, his son says, but I have got you something. Got something for you.

Martin looks down. He studies his naked feet.

I hate new shoes, he says. Just look at that blister. Don't tell me you've made something. Not another pot. I couldn't bear it. Don't they teach you anything else?

His son says, Not another pot. At the moment I don't have time. O-levels. In case you've forgotten.

Martin says, I haven't forgotten. Resits. The shame of it. So when am I going to get it, this gift?

His son says, Tonight. After school. Jane has dinner planned. For nine, I think. So there's plenty of time.

Martin says, That blazer is none too clean.

His son says, Your dressing gown has seen better days. More coffee?

Martin closes his dressing gown, and belts it.

Sorry, he says.

No need, his son says. I've seen it all before. I'll get the coffee.

How old are you, Fred? Martin says. Sorry to ask.

I have no sense of time either, Fred says. I'm fifteen. And a half. How old are you?

A yell, muffled by distance and closed doors, is heard.

Martin says, She wakes.

Fred says, Saved by the bell. I can always ask her, you know.

What makes you think, Martin says, that I told her the truth?

They smile.

Oh well, Fred says. It was worth a try.

I was twenty when you were born, Martin says. Where's your calculator?

This conversation, Fred says, is getting a bit father-and-son. Not to say schoolmasterly. You'd better get back to Jane.

Martin says, Where are the cats?

That reminds me, Fred says. Jane asked me to remind you to check and see if they've put your ad up yet.

I suppose I'd better, Martin says. I shall miss their miasmal presence. Where have they puked this morning? Not on the records again?

There is another yell from upstairs. This time it is more distinct. The monosyllable Fred! is audible.

I couldn't find any, Fred says. I suppose they do have to go?

It's either them or Jane, Martin says. We can't have her crying all the time. But a new home. Not put down, I promise.

Bags under the eyes, Fred says. Oh well. Fair exchange, I suppose. I like her.

We hear the sound of an upstairs door opening and closing, and the sound of a voice from the head of the stairs.

Fred, you bastard, the voice says. I asked you to wake me. It's Martin's birthday.

Dulcet tones, Fred says.

Martin stands up.

Change your blazer, he says. There's a dear.

OK, Fred says.

Martin goes to the kitchen door and shouts, Go back to bed. I'm still here. He turns back into the kitchen.

Time for her coffee, he says.

Fred pours coffee into Martin's cup and hands it over the bar.

Was it fun? he says. The cockring.

OK, Martin says. I'll see you tonight.

I hope so, Fred says.

Martin takes the coffee cup, and goes back upstairs. He pushes open the bedroom door with his foot, crinkles his nose against the smell of sleep, and enters. What, for lack of a better word, we will call his girlfriend, sits propped by pillows.

Happy birthday darling, she says.

Martin says, Bleary and beautiful, puts the coffee on the floor by the bed, and leans down to kiss her. She encircles his neck with her arms, and pulls herself into a kneeling position. She kisses him explosively on the ear.

Don't kiss my ear, he says. I don't like having my goddamn ear kissed. It hurts. It echoes.

Jane says, Crabby and beautiful. I love you.

She hugs him. He kisses her. First on the lips, then on each breast.

Time to get dressed, he says.

Not yet, she says, and leans over to fish under the bed. Martin takes this opportunity to kiss her buttocks. She pulls an enormous parcel out from under the bed. With expressions of rapture Martin unwraps the parcel to reveal the brown fur-lined overcoat already mentioned.

Holy mackerel! Martin says. Wherever did you get it? It's stunning.

He takes off his dressing gown and puts the overcoat on.

I'm going to be unbelievably late, he says. How do I look?

Stunning, Jane says. Why not let's be very late?

Uh-uh, Martin says. Tonight.

He takes off the overcoat.

OK, Jane says. Dinner at nine.

She stands by the bed and opens her arms. Jane and Martin embrace. Shortly they release each other, and Jane gets back into bed. Martin goes to the wardrobe and speedily dresses. Jane sniffs and wipes her eyes.

Cats, Martin says. I'll check the ad today. Bye.

Bye, Jane says. What is it tonight? Fashion or fucking?

Fucking, Martin says. But I won't be late.

I love you, Jane says.

Good, Martin says.

Yes, Jane says. Very good.

You're beautiful, Martin says.

I know, Jane says.

Two

The journey from Notting Hill Gate, where we saw him first, to Embankment has been accomplished. Martin has spent most of it with a disregarded letterpad, of which more later, open on his knees. The pad was disregarded because Martin is worried by his vision. Recently, he cannot say exactly when, he has become conscious of a flaw in his right eye – the eye, incidentally, which is not short-sighted. He attributes this flaw to some sort of fleck on his pupil which causes a minute but irritating dot to dance between him and the world. He tends to concentrate on this dot, and has succeeded in training his eyes, and the dot with them, into immobility. He is not unaware of the look of pleasant abstraction that this immobility lends his features. An interesting side effect of this condition is that he now feels unable to pass his journey in the oblivion of reading or writing, and, although he still carries a book or a letterpad, he rarely uses them. Rather to his surprise, as he has always considered himself the sort of person that dreads an unfilled moment, he finds he welcomes the opportunity for increased contemplation that this lack of occupation affords him. This morning's journey was spent rehearsing certain words of advice and consolation he intends to write to one of his friends who is on the brink of separation from his wife. Hence the letterpad. He repeats to himself choice words and phrases as he walks from Embankment to Charing Cross mainline station. He does this in an effort to commit them to memory, although experience has taught him that, when confronted with a white sheet of paper, his mind will prove as blank as the paper. In this connection he cherishes a passage from a novel by the late Michael Ayrton, in which the rape of a white sheet of paper is mentioned, and the need to justify that rape by ensuring that one's writing is more beautiful than the blankness. This concept enables him to label his disability as reticence. In his more honest moments he admits that this is self-deception. He would, in fact, give his eye teeth, or maybe something less conspicuous, such as his little toe, for the ability to transfer his thoughts to paper with felicity. This is a greater sacrifice than would at first appear, as he is excited by feet in general, and his own in particular.

At the station bookshop he buys a *Times Literary Supplement*, a *Times Educational Supplement*, a copy of *Quarto*, the December edition of *Gramophone*, for the critics' choice and an article on early music, an *Uomo in Vogue*, and a *Films Illustrated*. He flips through, but rejects, *Private Eye*, a Wodehouse omnibus, *Harper's Bazaar*, and a newly published paperback biography of Trotsky.

He is an avid buyer of printed matter, and can rarely pass a news-agent's without an effort of will. He will be late for an appointment this evening, for instance, because he will spend half an hour browsing through the French section of Grant and Cutler. This morning, however, because of his rejection of the mentioned works, he congratulates himself on a comparatively cheap escape.

He is successful in his search for a single compartment to himself on the train, and settles down, not without some conflict, in the left-hand seat facing forwards, to await its departure. His choice of seat is a recurring problem. He can never decide whether he prefers the east or the west view from Hungerford Bridge, and as he regards either of these views as among the most rewarding in London, the question is of some importance to him. Certainly he finds the effect of taking off into the air that is caused by the train's leaving the station inspiriting enough to make him forego his usual preference for sitting with his back to the engine.

The river crossing past, he turns his attention to the letterpad.

Damn, he writes, I've forgotten to take my kelp pills. I shall be grouchy all day. And my face will go blotchy if I'm not careful, which will be a bore as I have an engagement this evening. Still, I won't dwell on it because I know you disapprove of all that.

I know you want me to advise you, but I am unbelievably reluctant to do it. One thing that being a teacher has taught me is that one should never, never, give advice. People don't need it, or really want it. And if you haven't already made up your mind, it would be an impertinence anyway. The only thing I can, or am going to, say is: Do what you want. Unblinkered. When you've decided what it is you want, do it. And take what follows. It is rent. What you must pay for following what you desire. But it is very important that you do so in the full knowledge of what you will suffer in either event. Whatever happens you will be miserably lonely, or miserable in company. And believe me, however it may appear in your present state, living alone is difficult. The grass is not greener. The important things – feeling hellish in the mornings, wintry afternoon teas, waiting for buses – are so much less important if you can't share them. And yet, if the orange is squeezed dry remember that Christ did not blast the barren fig tree for nothing. And, whatever you do, do not confuse your love for one person with your love for another. That's why it is always a mistake to have children in an attempt to keep a marriage together. All right, keep your shirt on. I'm not suggesting that that's what you did. But you do have a child, my dear, and to stay with Steph because you love him is an insult to both of them, and to you. I know, I know. I'm lucky. I had it both ways. But I paid my rent. Fred is with me because Katy died, so I guess you could say that she paid her rent too. He sends his love, by the way. Fred does. Jane too. And if you think this display of family solidarity is just rubbing salt in your wounds, remember that Steph is my friend too. And I would give, probably shall give, her the same lack of advice that I give you. Ultimately one has only one loyalty, to honesty, and if this test has arrived, if you have to give up your wife, or your son, or both, then you should be glad. Yes, glad. Because it wouldn't be honest to keep them, or rather because keeping them is what you would be doing, rather than freely sharing with them. And I think that that is probably enough in-depth emotion for one morning. Remember, remember dear, that I love you, and so does Fred, and we love Steph too. You are the base from which we wander. And you are not to hurt each other, especially not in the name of anything, and if separation is the way forward, take it. Separate. And now, as I seem to be close to giving what I said I wouldn't, I'm going to stop.

Martin sits and rests his eyes. The train slows down, and he closes the letterpad and puts it into the fishing bag. The train pulls up at a station which, in Martin's words, shall remain nameless, out of respect for the dead. With a well but not perfectly concealed anxiety he first taps, then investigates, his pockets for keys, season ticket, wallet, chequebook. He is a compulsive checker of the almost certain, and has been known to get up in the middle of the night to verify that the television is unplugged, the bathroom window open, or the front door properly locked. This done, he recrooks the umbrella into his pocket, slings the fishing bag over his shoulder, and alights.

Hi, he says to the ticket collector.

Morning, the ticket collector says, Funny old colour.

Martin looks around and becomes conscious of two things in quick succession. First, that it is a beautiful morning, the light a clear brumous yellow. Second, and not for the first time, that he is the sort of person who doesn't notice that sort of thing until it is pointed out to him.

Yes, he says. Lovely isn't it?

Disco Annie, who is waiting for him outside the station, winds down the car window and says, My God, what have you got on? You look like a fashion plate.

I am a fashion plate, Martin says. More often than not.

Don't tell me, Disco Annie says. You stole it from Wardrobe.

It's a present, Martin says, getting into the car. From Jane. Though if she stole it from Wardrobe I wouldn't be surprised.

Disco Annie starts the car and moves into the traffic.

Sorry, she says. I forgot.

Don't worry, Martin says. I'm too old to care.

I'll buy you a drink at lunch, Disco Annie says. If there's time.

Why not? Martin says.

Actually, Disco Annie says, there probably won't be. I'm having trouble.

She stops the car at a red light.

Boy trouble, she says. Paul d'Acosta.

Again, Martin says.

Still, Disco Annie says. We saw the educational psychiatrist yesterday. Not much help. We are to make no educational allowances. Whatever that may mean.

The light changes to green. Disco Annie winds down the window.

Come on, she shouts to the car in front. It's not going to get any greener.

He can't stop, she says, once they are moving again. He doesn't know why he does it. It will be gaol this time, I expect. They found over two thousand quid's worth of electrical goods under his bed. God knows where he got them from. He won't say. The

175

police are being nice but firm. I was wondering if you'd speak to him.

What the hell can I say? Martin says.

I don't know, Disco Annie says. I've tried everything. He doesn't handle women well, the shrink says.

I'm not surprised, Martin says. She's a ten valium a day mother, you know. Before breakfast.

Yes, Disco Annie says. And I remind him of her. Would you believe? Which makes me worse than useless. Such nonsense. Will you? Speak to him. Please, Bear.

OK, Martin says. But I can't imagine what good it will do.

Lunchtime? Disco Annie says.

Half-past twelve, Martin says. After physical jerks.

Happy birthday Bear, Disco Annie says.

Thanks, Martin says. Thanks a million.

I'll buy you a drink sometime, Disco Annie says.

Three

Martin lies on his back on the horse and lifts weights into the air.

Thirty-nine, he says.

It is midday.

Forty, he says. Forty-one. Forty-two.

Shut up and pump, Grace Poole says.

Forty-three, Martin says. Forty-four. Of course I was not always as you see me now. Forty-eight.

Forty-seven, Grace Poole says.

Forty-eight, Martin says. For. Ty. Nine.

Get it up, Grace Poole says. Push, you stuck-up, cocky bastard. Push.

Martin holds the weight at full extension.

Grace, he says. Please. There are children present.

Shut up and pump, Grace Poole says. Ten more.

Shit, Martin says. I'll never do it. Fifty-one. Fifty-two. Fifty-three.

Come on sir, a voice says.

Fifty-four. Fifty-five. Fifty-six, Martin says.

Push sir, another voice says, and another voice, more daring, Get it up.

Fifty-seven. Fifty-eight. Fifty-nine, Martin says. Christ, I'll never do it.

Get your finger out and shove, Grace Poole says.

Six. Ty! Martin says. Someone take the goddamn thing. Quick.

Schoolboy hands divest him of the weight. He lies, eyes closed, panting.

Not bad, Grace Poole says. If you cared as much for your body as you do for the cut of your tracksuit you'd be OK. Wallbars next. Thirty.

Bitch, Martin says.

Please, a boy's voice says. There are children present.

Martin goes to the wallbars. He climbs and hangs, facing outward. He lifts his knees to his chin.

Christ, a voice to his left says, and the thief.

Martin turns to see Paul d'Acosta similarly positioned. They lift their knees to their chin.

Hi kid, Martin says. Half-past, right? My place. Miss Maitland tell you?

Yes, the boy says. She informed me.

They lift their knees again.

I'm off, Paul d'Acosta says.

He drops from the wallbars.

See you in the showers, Martin says.

Not if I see you first, Paul d'Acosta says.

Martin looks after the retreating boy, then continues his exercise.

Spring jumps next, Grace Poole says. Then back to the weights.

Grace, I have only one life, Martin says. I have an interview.

You'll be late, Grace Poole says. Get a move on.

I'm going to be sick, Martin says.

Not in my gym you're not, Grace Poole says. Get on with it.

Yes matron. Yes nurse, Martin says. Yes Grace Poole.

He gets on with it.

Twenty minutes later, comfortably tired, his hair still wet from the shower, he enters his classroom. Paul d'Acosta stands by his desk, looking out of the window. He does not move when Martin enters, or redirect his gaze.

Hi kid, Martin says.

Name's Paolo, Paul d'Acosta says.

Sorry, Martin says. Force of habit. I'm nice to everybody.

He sits at his desk.

Do you want to sit down? he says. Or would you rather look out of the window?

Paul d'Acosta turns into the room and sits, with apparent unconcern, on the edge of Martin's desk. Martin opens the desk drawer and takes out cigarettes, matches, and an ashtray.

Smoke? he says.

Paul d'Acosta shrugs, then takes the proffered cigarette. Martin takes one for himself and lights both.

Thanks, he says.

Sorry, Paul d'Acosta says. Thanks. Sir.

Well, Martin says. I guess you know what this is all about.

You're not, Paul d'Acosta says. Nice to everyone. You treat everyone in the same way. That's not the same thing. Not with everyone. That means you don't care. You don't care enough to be not nice. Even when it's deserved.

And who decides, Martin says, what is deserved?

You use your niceness like a weapon, Paul d'Acosta says. That's not nice.

What purpose would it serve, Martin says, if I were nasty? Would it make you feel better? A satisfying scene, is that what you want? Tears and slamming of doors. Grand opera stuff, Paolo?

Very clever, Paul d'Acosta says.

Well is it? Martin says. A punishment. Is that what you want?

So I'm a masochist, Paul d'Acosta says. That makes it easier. OK. I guess in a way. But it's got to come from someone who cares.

Martin inhales cigarette smoke, and gently exhales.

I mean, Paul d'Acosta says, it's not as if I'm not. Punished. Five times in court. God knows how many good thrashings. My mum cries, and takes pills, and says she's going to kill herself.

You sound, Martin says, almost proud of it all.

But it doesn't mean anything, Paul d'Acosta says. They don't care. It's their morality that's outraged. Their lives that are ruined.

So no one else, Martin says, is allowed any scenes?

They can do what they like, Paul d'Acosta says. They don't fool me. They don't care about me.

And Miss Maitland? Martin says. What about her?

She gets paid, Paul d'Acosta says. And she shoves it off on to you anyway.

And I'm supposed to care, Martin says. Is that it?

I don't know, Paul d'Acosta says. That's what we're here to find out, isn't it?

I can't see anything to care about, Martin says. Who do you care about after all?

No bargains, Paul d'Acosta says. I can look after myself.

Right into gaol, Martin says.

I can look after myself, Paul d'Acosta says.

Then I don't see what I can do, Martin says. You don't want any help.

I didn't say that, Paul d'Acosta says. Just because I can look after myself doesn't mean I want to have to. I want to decide who I want to help me.

Martin stubs out his cigarette. Paul d'Acosta pinches off the end of his and puts the butt into his pocket.

And how, Martin says, do I prove myself? Always assuming that I want to. No bargains, my ass. You're treating me to a pretty hefty slice of blackmail here.

Yes, Paul d'Acosta says. I am, aren't I?

Smug bastard, Martin says.

Smug bastard shit, Paul d'Acosta says. I've got a lot to lose here.

And you're also laying a whole lot more on me, Martin says,

than you have any right to. What makes you think I'm interested in why, or even if, you steal? What makes you think I could give a damn whether you go to gaol or not?

Well you're here, aren't you? Paul d'Acosta says.

At Miss Maitland's request, Martin says. I'm doing the job I'm paid to. Like her.

Yes, Paul d'Acosta says. Just like her. That's why she's having lunch and you're here. With me.

You're reading too much into things, Martin says. I care just about as much as she does. Which is just about midway between how much you care, and how much you'll allow us to care. All we are is teachers, you know. Though we do know enough about amateur psychiatry to recognize a standard manoeuvre when we see one. You're pushing us to rejection point so that you can have a couple more people to blame. Poor Paolo. Sure I'm here with you. And you are fighting damned hard to ensure that I'm wasting my time.

Valuable time, Paul d'Acosta says. I'm sorry to be so ordinary.

What's the point of being sorry? Martin says. Any fool can admit his mistake. There's no virtue in the admission if you make no effort to change. You're making me sound like a teacher, Paolo, you're forcing me into your mould. And I resent it. And I'm not letting you get away with it. All right. No bargains. You want to be a loser, be a loser. Sod off then, and leave me out of it.

Kiss me, Paul d'Acosta says. You're beautiful when you're angry.

He stands up laughing, and moves round the desk. Martin stands up and faces him, also laughing.

You don't fool me, Paul d'Acosta says.

Martin stops laughing.

I'm sorry, he says, let's call it a good joke, and leave it at that.

Paul d'Acosta stops laughing.

I'm not blind, he says, and I'm not a fool.

OK Paolo, Martin says. You can go now. This isn't getting us anywhere.

Kiss me, Paul d'Acosta says. I mean it. Joke over. Please Bear.

Shit, Martin says. Go away. Go read a good book or something.

Magazines, Paul d'Acosta says. I read magazines.

He steps closer to Martin and closes his eyes. Martin doesn't move. After a while the boy opens his eyes and grabs Martin round the waist.

I want you to fuck me, he says. I want to suck your cock.

Martin concentrates his gaze on the wall behind Paul d'Acosta's head. The boy moves his hands from Martin's waist to the back of his head. He grasps Martin's hair and kisses him. The kiss lands on the corner of Martin's mouth. Martin does not move, continues staring at the wall. The boy releases him and walks to the door. Martin sits down at his desk. At the door Paul d'Acosta turns back, opens his mouth to speak, but is prevented.

See you around, kid, Martin says.

Not if I see you first, Paul d'Acosta says.

After the boy has gone, Martin continues sitting for some time. Then he opens his desk drawer, looking for his cigarettes. They are neither in the drawer nor on the desk nor anywhere to be seen. He takes a deep breath. Disco Annie enters.

I'm sorry, she says.

How much of that did you catch? Martin says.

Enough to know it didn't work, Disco Annie says.

The little bastard stole my cigarettes, Martin says.

An impossible child, Disco Annie says. Have one of mine.

Never again, Martin says.

Until the next time, Disco Annie says.

A hundred and one things a boy can do, Martin says. Where's that cigarette? I need a bath.

And a drink, Disco Annie says, lighting their cigarettes. I owe you one, don't forget.

Four

Five and a half hours later Martin, half an hour in Grant and Cutler behind him, rings the bell of a house in Floral Street. It is snowing. An aria by Verdi floats from an open upper window.

Martin stamps his feet as he waits, and spins his umbrella to dislodge snowflakes. The entryphone says hello, and Martin gives his name and pushes the door open. He is immediately enveloped in heat. Tia Juana likes people to sweat.

Come up darling, an upstairs voice calls above the Verdi. You're late.

Martin removes his outer layer.

Sorry, he says. Trains. Isn't this the most sod awful weather. I'm taking my shoes off.

Tia Juana has come to the head of the stairs.

Why not darling? he says. It all comes off in the end. Your umbrella is dripping on my carpet.

I am dripping on your carpet, you *House and Garden* queen, Martin says.

Tia Juana meditates.

Peevish, he says, and makes for his sitting room.

Martin follows him, shaking his head.

And I'm speckling your wallpaper with my sodden curls, he says.

Verdi climaxes as he enters Tia Juana's sitting room.

Perfect timing, Tia Juana says. As usual. That's why I like you.

Amore Vincera, Martin says. Appropriate, do you think?

Allow an actress her illusions, Tia Juana says. Sherry?

La Fanciulla del West End, Martin says.

It's on the cabinet, Tia Juana says. Sweet and sticky. Just for you.

Treacle, Martin says, pouring golden oloroso. Yum yum!

Now, dear Bear, Tia Juana says. Business.

Juana, Martin says. Curb your impatience. I'm tired.

You're looking, Tia Juana says, not the better for wear. You must be careful. We can't afford it.

We can afford, Martin says, damn near anything we want. I'm a gold mine, and don't you forget it.

Bills, Tia Juana says, bills.

You could turn the heating down, Martin says.

Not that sort of bill, Tia Juana says. Naïve child.

Naïf, Martin says. I'm older than you are.

And a teacher too, Tia Juana says. Such a skilful girl.

Don't you ever tire, Martin says, of all this campery? These are the eighties, darling. Mae West is dead.

We are all liberated, Tia Juana says. What an unbuttoned sisterhood we are. Now get that sherry down you, girl, and let's get to it.

Martin carries his full sherry glass across the room, and sits next to Tia Juana on the sofa.

Could we turn it down? he says. Or off preferably.

Tia Juana rises from the sofa, turns down Verdi, and takes an envelope from his desk.

Contact sheets, he says. Last Friday and Monday.

Friday I recall was not a success, Martin says. I told you he was wrong. The story line was pretty tacky too. I don't make a good trucker.

Art, Tia Juana says, is long. And he was long.

He hands the contact sheets to Martin, and reseats himself. Martin sips sherry, and studies the sheets.

He looks at his own cock too much, he says. He gives the game away.

Your lack of interest, Tia Juana says, is not apparent.

Art, Martin says. Well let's see what can be salvaged.

He extracts a pen from his pocket, and circles and crosses the sheet.

Not much, he says. It'll do as illustrations. It won't stand up on its own. Let's have a look at Monday.

Monday, Tia Juana says, is good.

Yes, Martin says. I remember. But not comfortable. I never want to kneel on a billiard table again. I got flat knees.

The facial expression, Tia Juana says, is marvellous.

Art, Martin says. The trick is to mix pain and pleasure in just the right proportion, and just a dash of surprise.

He inspects the sheet closely.

Art in this case, he says, was helped considerably by nature. I see it brought tears to the eyes. They'll do. Except for this one.

I look drunk. Or doped. Or both. What can I have been doing?

Struggling for air by the look of it, Tia Juana says.

Well, Martin says. What have you got for me tonight?

Tia Juana places his fingertips together.

Tonight, he says, is special. He says he's nineteen. I would guess sixteen.

Boys, Martin says, are rarely clean. I hope you've soaped him.

He's with Pearl now, Tia Juana says.

What's his cock like? Martin says. Clean? Circumcised?

Both, Tia Juana says. He's tall, curly hair, skinny. What are you going to do?

Martin meditates.

The best part, he says, of a boy's body is where the thigh joins the trunk. The lines, you know. And the backsweep to the buttocks.

Yes, Tia Juana says. What are you going to do?

The thing is, Martin says, you must reverse expectation. I shall fuck him, of course. My public expects it. Then he can fuck me. That drives them wild. Bitch fucks butch. And whatever takes my fancy over and above. Depending on how pretty he is.

Not my type, Tia Juana says. I prefer the older type. Pearl, by the way, has a new assistant. Not a pretty sight. But a wizard with lights.

Martin drains his glass.

OK, he says. Time to go upstairs. What's the story line? No shower work please. All that soap. Scoutmaster stuff, I guess, considering the age.

Play it by ear, Tia Juana says. Not scoutmaster stuff, I think. Bearing in mind the disappointed expectation.

Missionary stuff, Martin says. About an hour? I have to get home.

As long as you like, Tia Juana says. See Pearl. But make it good.

Don't I always, Martin says. When have I ever let you down?

Or him, Tia Juana says. When have you ever let him down?

You're getting sentimental in your middle age, Martin says.

I'm younger than you, Tia Juana says.

Tia Juana's bathroom, to which Martin now repairs, is a spacious venetian-blinded room painted canary yellow, plentifully supplied with tropical plants, of which not a few hang in macrame-slung pottery bowls from the ceiling, and a variety of specialized washing fitments. Martin makes for the mirror, a full length bamboo-surrounded cheval-glass, before which he undresses. For as long as he can remember he has had an aversion, which he considers pathological, to lavatories. He therefore habitually urinates into the sink. On this occasion he is interrupted in mid-pee by Pearl Fisher's entry.

Sorry Pearl, he says.

Don't worry about it, Pearl Fisher says. Stranger things happen in this room.

Martin finishes his pee, and adjusts his cockring, under Pearl Fisher's appraising eye.

I shall give myself a callous, he says, at this rate. Will I do?

A bit of sponge work, Pearl Fisher says. Come and stand in the light.

Martin stands in the light. Pearl Fisher expertly handles sponges and brushes.

There, she says. Everything's ready. When you are.

In a minute, Martin says. I must gather my resources.

Pearl Fisher gustily sighs.

You and me both, she says. It's been a long day. You are the third since lunch.

She sits on the edge of the bath. Martin returns his attention to the mirror.

You're a genius, Pearl, he says.

He's a nice kid, Pearl Fisher says.

Jesus, Martin says. What is this? Have you and Juana got some sort of conspiracy going here? I shouldn't worry. He's probably been through it all before. We don't get many virgins through here, whatever Juana's handouts may say.

Do you enjoy your work? Pearl Fisher says.

Pearl, Martin says. This is one hell of a time for that sort of question. How many years have you been doing this?

I've known you for four, Pearl Fisher says. We've never spoken. Not so's you'd notice. You know that? In all that time we've never talked. Nothing but work. People get hurt you know.

I know Pearl, Martin says. You've got a heart of gold. Your heart is with the Baptist ladies' sewing guild, even as your hand creates schoolboy bedrooms, log cabins, haystacks, and changing rooms. And I'm a bastard. What is it today by the way?

Just straight bedroom stuff, Pearl Fisher says. A few navajo rugs. Very tasteful. I cannot say, Martin Conrad, that I like you very much.

Do you have to? Martin says. I just pay your bills. I just keep you in Gucci, Pucci, and Fiorucci. I and a few others, like three since lunch. Like your precious kid in there.

You're running, Pearl Fisher says. Come here.

Again she plies brushes and sponge. Downstairs, filtered by doors, Verdi gives way to Wagner.

Sorry, Pearl, Martin says.

Never mind, Pearl Fisher says. Temperament. By the way you're not to kiss his ear. He says he hates to have his goddamn ear kissed.

Shit, Martin says.

Funny that, Pearl Fisher says.

She gets up from the edge of the bath.

Ready when you are, she says.

Give me a bit, Martin says.

Wash the sink, Pearl Fisher says over her shoulder as she leaves.

Alone in the bathroom Martin takes a deep breath and counts to twenty. Then he walks next door into Tia Juana's enormous studio bedroom where, through banks of cameras and lights, over Pearl Fisher's dimpled shoulder, he sees, supine atop snowy linen and navajo rugs, Fred's unclothed figure. He walks to the bed.

Hi dad, Fred says.

Hi kid, Martin says.

Martin contemplates with decreasing detachment his son's glabrous nakedness. To his surprise, and here we must bear in mind his previous remarks on the adolescent physique, it is the sight of Fred's coltish knees that he finds particularly arresting. Fred stands up and moves to face his father. He hugs him, and plants a sherry-fragrant kiss on his cheek.

Happy birthday Bear, he says.

Martin returns his son's hug.

Thanks kid, he says.

Five

Un vendredi pas comme les autres, Fred says. Taxi? We're running a bit short on time.

Martin closes Tia Juana's door behind them and peers through the snow.

Taxi, he says. If we can get one. How long do we have?

Fred takes his father's hand and holds it.

About half an hour I think, he says. Come on. We'll pick one up in Charing Cross Road.

Hand in hand they stumble over the impacted snow. In St Martin's Lane Fred slips and falls, almost pulling Martin over with him. They laugh, right themselves, and walk on. At Cambridge Circus Martin disengages his hand from his son's and puts it in his pocket.

Numb, he says.

There's a taxi, Fred says, and runs forward waving.

Martin quickly bunches a snowball and throws it at Fred's back. Fred stops the taxi and gives directions. As they settle into the cab Martin hands Fred an envelope. Fred inspects the contents and hands them back to Martin.

Very nice, he says.

Martin puts the photographs back into the envelope.

We look as if we enjoyed ourselves, he says. That's the main thing.

We did, didn't we? Fred says. I'm tired.

He lies back and closes his eyes. After a while Martin does the same. The taxi makes a slow snowbound progress. It is impossible to say whether they sleep or not, but let us assume that they do. At Chepstow Villas the driver rouses them. They pay him and get out into the snow. As Martin is turning into his pathway a snowball hits him on the back of his head. For several minutes Fred and Martin pelt each other with snowballs, laughing and gasping with cold. Then, wet-haired and, let us suppose, happy, they enter their house. They stamp their feet in the hall. Martin calls, Jane we're back. Jane comes out into the hall.

Hi kids, she says.

Martin and Jane embrace. Fred and Jane kiss. They enter the sitting room. A champagne cork pops. A roomful of people sings Happy Birthday.

Surprise surprise! everybody says.